TRIPLE TROUBLE PLUS ONE

BOOK 4

ANYTHING IS POSSIBLE!

by
Diane C. Wander

Printed in the United States of America
First Printing, 2019

ISBN: 978-0-9970558-7-0 (Paperback Edition)

This novel is a work of fiction. Where some of the characters are based in part on the personalities of real people, the names and incidents are fictitious. Where the settings are based on real places, the incidents that take place at these settings are the product of the author's imagination and are used fictitiously.

<u>Dedication</u>

For every educator who guides, motivates, and inspires students to want to learn…

❧

For every teacher whose inexhaustible energy, persistence, and passion enable students to achieve the goals they set for themselves…

❧

Thank you for making a difference in the lives of each and every student and helping them to realize that

<u>Anything is Possible</u>!

TABLE OF CONTENTS

The New Kids on the Block

It was the last Sunday…the final weekend…the unwelcomed end to the very best summer ever! After seven amazing weeks at sleepaway camp and ten lazy, fun-filled days at home, the Hoffman kids were going back to school. Twelve-year-old Rebecca Hoffman was sitting on the family room couch flipping channels on the remote while her ten-year-old sister Maddie played *Roblox* on her iPad.

Why can't summer be ten months and school only two months? Rebecca thought to herself. *I would do anything for just one more week of sleepaway camp…just one more week of no homework…just one more week of….*

"Thump! Thump! Thump!"

Rebecca's thoughts came to a halt. Hearing the sounds of dribbling basketballs, Rebecca walked to the family room window and opened it. Outside, her brothers, Jason and Brayden, were playing basketball.

Rebecca and her two brothers were triplets. Because they were fraternal, they did not look anything alike. Where Brayden had brown hair, blue eyes, and wore glasses, Jason was shorter and skinnier, with spiky brown hair and brown eyes. Rebecca was also skinny, with red curly hair, brown eyes, and lots of freckles. Their ten-year-old younger sister Maddie had long brown braids, brown eyes, and wore glasses like Brayden.

"Hey!" said Rebecca. "Who's that kid with the boys?"

"What kid?" asked Maddie.

"Some boy playing basketball with Jason and Brayden in our driveway. He keeps running around in circles and shouting."

As much as Maddie did not want to be interrupted in the middle of her game, she put down her iPad and ran to the window.

"I won! I won! 21! 21!" the boy shouted. Holding the basketball like it was a trophy, he weaved in and out around Jason and Brayden.

"Why's he doing that?" asked Maddie.

"Got me," said Rebecca.

Maddie returned to the couch while Rebecca continued to watch the new boy shout and make circles around Jason and Brayden. Just as she started to resume her game of *Roblox*, Rebecca interrupted her once again.

"Look, Maddie! Now there are two girls walking up our driveway, and the younger one has an American Girl doll just like you!"

Maddie jumped up immediately. The biggest smile came across her face because she loved American Girl dolls. Hers was actually named Maddie and even looked like her. Maddie went upstairs, grabbed her doll, and ran back down as fast as she could. "Come on, Rebecca," she shouted. "We've gotta meet them!"

With all thoughts of watching TV and playing video games forgotten, Rebecca and Maddie ran outside to meet the new kids on the block.

❧

"I won! I won! 21! 21!" the new boy screamed again.

Maddie and Rebecca walked towards the basketball court.

"Hey! Why do you keep screaming like that?" asked Maddie. "Stop already!"

Suddenly the new boy stopped screaming and froze in place. He looked startled. Thinking she might have come across as rude, Maddie decided to apologize. But before she could get the words out, her older brother Jason jumped in.

"It's okay, Jake. This is my younger sister Maddie and my triplet sister Rebecca. Rebecca's the same age as Brayden and me."

"Hi, Jake," said Maddie. "Sorry I snapped at you. Actually, I'm really happy you're here. No one ever beats Jason and Brayden!"

Maddie and Rebecca both laughed. "Go, Jake!" they shouted at the same time.

"Go, Jake! Go, Jake!" echoed Jake, in a robot-like voice.

At the edge of the driveway, the two new girls stood quietly and watched. They were Jake's sisters, Jordie and Leah. Jordie was Jake's twin, and Leah was their younger sibling. Knowing that Jake would keep yelling unless he was distracted, Jordie took Leah's hand and walked towards the basketball court.

"Hi! I'm Jordie Green," she said to the Hoffman kids. "Jake and I are twins." Jordie put her hand on Jake's arm and smiled at him. "We're 11. How old are you?"

"Jason, Brayden, and me are 12," said Rebecca. "We're triplets but not *identical.* We're *fraternal.*"

"We're *fraternal,* too," said Jordie, as she pointed to Jake. "We don't look alike either."

Jake and Jordie had blue eyes and red curly hair and were both thin, but Jake was much taller than his sister. Their younger sister, Leah, had long brown braids and brown eyes.

"Can you believe that twins and triplets are living across the street from each other?" asked Rebecca. "That is so cool!"

"Very cool, Rebecca," her sister Maddie said sarcastically. "Did you forget about me?" Maddie turned towards the two new girls. "I'm Maddie, the *triplets'* younger sister. I'm 10."

"And I'm Leah, the *twins'* younger sister. I'm 9, and I always get forgotten, too."

"Hey! The two of you look alike!" Brayden exclaimed, as he stared at his sister Maddie and the Green's younger sister Leah. "Look, Jason. They both have long brown braids and brown eyes. They even have the same kind of doll."

Both Leah and Maddie clutched their American Girl dolls and smiled from ear to ear.

"And what about them?" said Jason, pointing to Rebecca, Jake, and Jordie. "They look alike, too." Jake and Jordie Green both had red curly hair. So did Rebecca, Jason and Brayden's triplet sister.

"Amazing!" Brayden exclaimed.

"What's amazing?" asked Mrs. Hoffman, as she walked across the driveway to the basketball court.

"Mom!" shouted Jason. "Check out the Green kids who moved in across the street. Maddie looks just like Leah… and Rebecca has red curly hair like Jake and Jordie. Isn't that funny?"

"Yes, I noticed that, too, when I met Jake, Jordie, and Leah."

"When did you meet them?" asked Brayden.

"This past week at a parent and student meeting at my school. Jake and Jordie will be together in the same fifth grade class there this year," Mrs. Hoffman said with a smile.

Mrs. Hoffman was a sixth grade Language Arts and Social Studies teacher at The Pathways School. The Hoffman kids, however, went to Royal Palm Academy. Brayden and Jason were going into seventh grade, Rebecca into sixth, and Maddie into fifth. Although Brayden, Rebecca, and Jason were all the same age, they were not in the same grade. Rebecca was one year behind her brothers because of difficulties she had with learning to read and write when she was younger.

"What about you, Leah?" asked Maddie. "Where are you going?"

"Royal Palm…just like you," she answered. "I'll be in 4th grade this year. I think we're gonna carpool with you in the afternoon, except on the days I go to gymnastics. I'm on the USAG Team."

"Me, too!" Maddie exclaimed.

Maddie beamed. She could not believe that Leah not only looked like her but also loved American Girl dolls, was on the USAG Team, and was going to the same school.

"I'm so glad you're all here!" Mrs. Hoffman gushed. "Let's celebrate. We have chocolate chip brownies that just came out of the oven."

"My dad makes the best brownies," bragged Rebecca. "He's a dentist but loves to bake. You gotta taste them!"

"Go brownies!" Jake chanted.

"Go brownies!" echoed Jason and Brayden.

As they all burst into laughter, they raced into the house hoping to be first in line for one of Dr. Hoffman's hot out of the oven chocolate chip brownies.

2

HAPPY WORDS

Twenty minutes later, the brownies were gone.

"I can't believe we ate 'em all!" Rebecca groaned as she, Maddie, Leah, and Jordie flopped down on the couch.

"Hey! Get off the couch," Brayden yelled. "Me, Jake, and Jason are gonna play basketball video games."

"No! We were here first! We want to watch TV. Mom!" shouted Rebecca. "Tell Brayden to move...."

Before Rebecca could finish, Mrs. Hoffman was standing right in front of the television. Knowing that her kids' quarreling over TV rights could go on forever, she had another idea in mind.

"Instead of watching TV, why don't you four girls go upstairs? I'm sure Jordie and Leah would love to see your rooms."

Maddie and Rebecca's eyes lit up. "Yes!" said Maddie. "Come on, Leah. I'll show you the new stuff I got for my Maddie doll."

"And Jordie has to see my new backpack," Rebecca added.

Maddie and Leah ran upstairs with Rebecca and Jordie right behind them. At the top of the stairwell, Maddie led

Leah into her room while Rebecca and Jordie entered Rebecca's. As their doors slammed shut, the sounds of dribbling basketballs, cheering crowds, and time out buzzers could be heard down below. Mrs. Hoffman breathed a sigh of relief knowing that all seven kids were happily occupied for however long that would last.

&

"I'm so glad you moved across the street," Rebecca said, as she jumped on her bed. "It's gonna be so much fun to have two more girls in the neighborhood. Jake's nice, but there are way too many boys around here. We need girl power!" Rebecca declared, as she raised her fist in the air.

Jordie started laughing but then suddenly got quiet.

"What's wrong, Jordie?"

Jordie sat down on the bed next to Rebecca but avoided looking at her. "I need to tell you something...something about Jake."

"What is it, Jordie?"

Jordie took a deep breath and then continued. "Jake's different. He does weird things."

"What kind of weird things?" asked Rebecca, although she kind of thought she knew the answer.

"Didn't you think it was weird when he kept repeating, '*I won! I won 21! 21!*' and kept spinning around?"

"I guess so, but I tried to ignore it. Besides, I hate the word *weird*. Lots of kids used to call me weird—even Jason, Brayden, and Maddie. They all made fun of me because I had trouble with reading and writing. When I had to read aloud in school, all the letters and words kept jumping around. So I messed up a lot, skipped words and even whole sentences. Everyone looked at me like I had some kind of disease!"

"Do you have *Dyslexia*?" asked Jordie.

"Yeah. How'd you know that?"

"Because I have the same thing. But you're lucky because you don't have it anymore."

"Yes I do!" said Rebecca. "Why do you think that?"

"Cuz you said that kids don't call you *weird* anymore."

"Just because they don't call me weird doesn't mean I don't have dyslexia. I read and write better than I used to, but I still have it, and my teachers say I'll always have it. Sometimes I get so frustrated because it takes me hours to do my homework. My brothers and sister are done in ten minutes. It's not fair!"

"It isn't fair!" Jordie repeated. "Leah is two years younger than me and always gets her work done way before I do. Mom says it's because I don't concentrate. I really try to pay attention, but it's so hard. Now I have to take a special pill every day to help me focus. That's because I have ADD—*Attention Deficit Disorder*."

"ADD? I think Jason and Brayden have that, too," said Rebecca. "Jason can't stop moving around for even one second, and Brayden always gets sidetracked from what he's doing. But I guess they're okay cuz they went to a special doctor, and he didn't give them any pills. Besides, they always do good in school. I had to stay back a year so I'm only in sixth. My mom says I was really sick when I was born. Since it took a long time for me to get healthy and strong, I had to have an extra year in school. Brayden and Jason were fine. They're so lucky," Rebecca said, sighing.

"Just like me and Jake. We were sick, too. We should be in sixth but are in fifth. It's just not fair." Jordie sat up and turned towards Rebecca. "Kids sometimes call me *weird*, too," she whispered. "I hate that. But I guess I'm luckier than Jake."

"Why are you luckier?" asked Rebecca.

"Because I don't act like Jake. The minute he opens his mouth, everyone thinks he's weird."

"Not *weird*!" Rebecca retorted. "*Different!*"

"*Different! Weird!* "What does it matter?" Jordie sighed and buried her face in her hands.

"Because **Words Matter**!" Rebecca insisted. "That's what my parents and teachers say. Good words make you feel happy. Bad words, like *weird*, make you sad."

Jordie looked up at Rebecca. "Do you have a word that makes you feel happy?"

Rebecca thought for a second, looked up at all the paintings on the walls of her room, and then smiled. "*Different!* That's my word," she said, as she pointed to a painting over her desk with the word *Different* in all the colors of the rainbow. I made that in art class. We had to pick a word that made us happy."

"Why'd you pick *different*?"

"*Different* is a good thing! No one else in my family can draw or paint like me. So, I'm different, and that makes me feel special. Mom says that every person has different things that they are good at and different things they're not so good at. Like you and me…we're not so good at reading and writing, but we're good at other things!"

"I'm good at ballet!" bragged Jordie. "Leah's good at gymnastics, and Jake is really good at basketball and doing math. He can do all kinds of math problems in his head. I can't do that."

"See!" Rebecca exclaimed. "Being different is a really good thing. Before I made that painting, I used to run down the stairs screaming for my mom every time my homework got too hard. Ever since my dad hung it over my desk, I don't do that so much anymore. My work is still tough, but when I look up at *different* and take a deep breath, the rainbows and multicolored letters calm me down."

"I want to feel like that too," said Jordie. "Can you make me a happy word? Jake should have one, too. Maybe it would help him stop spinning and saying things over and over again."

"What word would you pick?"

Jordie closed her eyes and started to think. Trying to picture the perfect word to put on her own bedroom wall, she imagined herself in ballet class spinning on one foot doing a pirouette.

"I got it," Jordie said, as she jumped off the bed. "But it's three words."

"What are they?"

"*On my toes!*"

"Why'd you pick those words?" asked Rebecca.

"In ballet class, our teacher always says that when we stand on our toes, we can reach for the stars and achieve anything we want."

Rebecca closed her eyes. "I can see it! Pink sparkly ballet slippers with stars around them. Do you want me to make you a picture?"

"Yes," said Jordie, as she hugged Rebecca. "You're my new best friend!"

Just then, Mrs. Hoffman called from the bottom of the stairs.

"Jordie…Leah…your mom wants you home."

"Wait! I've got to show you my backpack," Rebecca insisted. Grabbing her multicolored tie-dyed backpack from underneath her bed, she held it up. Jordie's eyes popped wide open.

"I can't believe it!" Jordie shouted. "I have the same exact one!"

"Red curly hair, dyslexia, and now backpacks!" exclaimed Rebecca.

"We're twins!" the girls said at the same exact time and started to laugh.

Rebecca and Jordie, followed by Maddie and Leah with American Girl dolls in hand, ran down the stairs where Jake was waiting.

"Home, Jordie. Home, Leah. Home now!" demanded Jake.

Jordie and Rebecca looked at each other as if they knew what they each were thinking. *"On Your Toes!"* shouted Rebecca. Jordie gave Rebecca a thumbs up, then ran out the door with her brother and sister.

*"On Your Toes…*what does that mean?" asked Jason.

"A secret code between friends!" Rebecca winked at Jason and then ran up the stairs to begin painting Jordie's happy words.

3

Pathways

As the sun set, the last few hours of summer vacation were just about over. The Hoffman foursome were in the family room packing their backpacks for the first day of school.

"Don't forget your summer reading books!" Mom shouted from the kitchen.

"Got them!" yelled Maddie and Rebecca. Jason and Brayden raced upstairs to find theirs.

Every summer, kids at Royal Palm Academy were required to read three books—two selected by the school and one that students could choose for themselves.

Upon return to the family room, the boys stuffed their books into their bags and zipped them closed. "Hey, Mom," said Jason. "Why aren't Jake and Jordie going to our school, like their sister Leah?"

Mrs. Hoffman walked into the family room, along with Dr. Hoffman. Knowing that she wanted to answer Jason's question in the right way, she paused to think about what she was going to say.

"Sit down, kids."

"Is this gonna take a long time?" Brayden grumbled. "We want our last hour of TV before the rules change." In the Hoffman house, there was only one hour of television on school nights, and that was only after homework was done.

"Not to worry, Brayden," Dr. Hoffman said. "You'll all get TV tonight. But Jason's question first. It's important!"

Brayden sighed and plopped down on the couch next to his sisters. Jason stretched himself out on the floor.

"Your new friends, Jake and Jordie, learn in *different* ways," Mom began.

"What does that mean?" asked Jason.

"We're all different and have things that we are good at and things that we're not so good at," she explained.

"Like Walt Disney!" declared Brayden. "He was a genius. But my teacher told us he had a hard time learning to read."

"That's right, Brayden. Walt Disney had *dyslexia*. So does Jordie."

"And me, too," said Rebecca.

"Yes, Rebecca. Both you and Jordie have difficulty with reading and writing. But Jordie also has ADD. She has a hard time with organization and remembering where she puts things."

"But you forgot to say what she's really good at," Rebecca said, interrupting. "Jordie's great at ballet!"

"What about Jake?" said Jason. "What's with him?"

"Jake has difficulty making friends and gets easily overwhelmed."

"Like when he kept spinning around and repeating himself?" Maddie asked.

18

"Yes," said Mom. "When Jake gets excited, he has trouble controlling his body and his words."

"But he's really good at basketball," Jason exclaimed. "His foul shots are amazing!"

"And Jordie says that he's great in math," added Rebecca.

"Yes, he is," Mom continued. "Jake and Jordie, like everybody, have things they do very well. But the things that are hard for them make it difficult for them to learn in a school like yours. So, they're going to The Pathways School, which has all kinds of programs. One of them is for students like Jake and Jordie, who learn differently."

"If I have dyslexia, how come I don't go to Pathways?" Rebecca asked.

"You've made so much progress, Rebecca. With your extra year in third grade and the special help you have received in reading since first grade, you're doing just fine at Royal Palm."

"But, it's not fair that the boys are always ahead of me. They'll be in seventh grade this year. I'm only in sixth! And Maddie's gonna be in fifth. She should be two years behind me, not one!"

"I know it's frustrating for you, Rebecca," Mom said, soothing her. "But think about how far you've come. You're doing so much better in school now. You get lots of A's and B's, and reading isn't as painful as it used to be. That extra year in school gave you the chance to strengthen your skills."

Dad walked over to Rebecca and put his arms around her. "Mom's right, Rebecca. We're so proud of everything you have accomplished. You should feel proud, too!"

Rebecca wanted to answer Dad, but she couldn't. She had a huge lump in her throat. She knew she should feel proud, but it was hard to feel proud when she compared herself to Jason and Brayden. *We're triplets!* she thought to herself. *I should be as smart as them!* Rebecca closed her eyes tight and took a deep breath. As if she were in her bedroom, she began to see the rainbow colors of her *different* painting vibrating in front of her. Suddenly, Rebecca's eyes popped wide open.

"I am proud!" she blurted out. "I'm proud of the way I draw and paint. Mrs. Owen, my art teacher, says I'm the best artist in her class. I know I'm getting better at reading and writing, but I'm really good in art, just like Jordie is in ballet and Jake in math and basketball."

"And what about the rest of us?" declared Maddie. "I made the USAG Team."

"And I'm really good at spelling," Brayden bragged.

"And you can't forget me!" Jason shouted. "I've ranked #1 in points per game in our Community Basketball League for the last four years!"

"But what about things you're not good at?" Rebecca said to her siblings. "You have them, too…like everyone else!"

Brayden, Jason, and Maddie got very quiet. The last thing they wanted to talk about was things they couldn't do well.

"You're right, Rebecca," Dad said, jumping in. "Everyone has something they can't do well. So, I'll start."

"But you're a dentist, and Mom's a teacher," Maddie said, interrupting. "You're good at everything!"

"No, Maddie, we're not good at everything," answered Dad. "But that doesn't mean I couldn't become a dentist, or Mom…a teacher. When I was a kid, I was terrible in all kind of sports, and I always got picked last for teams. That was really embarrassing. But even worse than that was my handwriting. Kids in my class made fun of me and used to say that my papers looked like a chicken stepped in ink and jumped all over the page. I still can't play sports, and I still have bad handwriting."

"Cluck, Cluck, Cluck! Cluck-Cluck!" Jason cackled as he bobbed his head like a chicken.

Everyone burst into laughter, even Dad. Jason was the comedian in the family and knew how to get everyone to laugh.

"What about you, Mom?" said Maddie.

"My memory," Mom answered. "Other kids could sit and listen to what the teacher was saying in class and remember everything. Not me! I always had to write it all down. I still do."

"Is that why you have post-it notes all over the place?" asked Rebecca.

"Not only post-it notes…. I have lots of lists and re-minders everywhere!"

"So now it's your turn," Dad said, as he looked at Brayden, Jason, and Maddie.

"I'll go first," announced Jason. "I can't sit still, and sometimes I say things I shouldn't say."

"Old news, bro," Brayden said sarcastically.

"Brayden…," warned Mrs. Hoffman. "We're proud of Jason. It's hard to admit you can't do something well. What about you?"

Brayden's face got red. He couldn't look his mother in the face but knew it was his turn to share. Brayden looked down at the floor and started to stutter.

"Well uh, uh, uh. I kinda get distracted a lot, especially when I have to write essays. I hate them! Even when I think I write something good, I can't read my own handwriting and have to start all over again. It makes me so angry!"

"I know how frustrating that feels," Dad said. "I guess we chicken script writers need to stick together!"

"Cluck, Cluck, Cluck! Cluck! Cluck!" This time, everyone ignored Jason, especially Maddie, who was next in line.

"My turn," said Maddie. Getting up from the couch, Maddie stared directly at Brayden, Jason, and Rebecca. "I used to hate it when you guys made fun of the way I talked. If it wasn't for speech therapy, you'd still be making fun of me."

"We didn't do that!" Jason and Brayden yelled.

"Yes you did, and so did Rebecca!"

"Enough, boys! Let Maddie finish," Mrs. Hoffman said.

Maddie paused for a second and then continued. "I can read and write okay, but sometimes I have a hard time understanding what I read. I hate comprehension questions!"

"But you've made so much progress," Mom said comforting her. "With the extra help you got last year during reading class, fifth grade will be so much easier for you."

Maddie looked away to hide the tears in her eyes. She hated the idea of being weak. Wiping her eyes with her sleeve, Maddie turned back to find her father standing right by her. He pulled her in for a hug.

"So we all have things that are hard for us to do," said Dr. Hoffman. "But that should never stop us. We just have to find a different path."

"Different path?" What does that mean, Dad?" asked Jason.

Dr. Hoffman sat down on the floor next to Jason. "Think about basketball," he replied. "When you're trying to get the ball to the basket, you need to move around the court looking for the right path. It's the same thing with everything we do. When something is difficult, we look for the right path to solve the problem. But not everyone takes the same path. Your path on the basketball court might be completely different from Jake's or Brayden's or from stars like LeBron James or Steph Curry. Rebecca's, Maddie's, and Jordie's paths with reading have also been different. Like in a race, we all get to the finish line but not at the same time or in the same way."

"So, every person needs to find the path that works best for them," Mom added. "That's what Jordie and Jake will learn how to do at Pathways."

"*The Pathways School!*" exclaimed Jason. "That's the perfect name. Everyone can choose different paths to help them learn. Cool!"

"And now we need to find the pathway to the TV," Dr. Hoffman declared. Who has the remote?"

"Right here," Brayden shouted, as he flipped it to Dad.

Within seconds, Dr. and Mrs. Hoffman and their fear-less foursome were cuddled up together for one last night of television before the start of school the very next day.

4

THE FIRST DAY OF SCHOOL BEGINS

Early Monday morning, the alarm on Jake Green's iPhone went off. Outside his window, it was still dark, and the moon was shining.

"Time to get up! Time to get up!" Jake shouted, as he ran into Jordie and Leah's rooms. They did not budge. Holding his phone in his hand, Jake rushed into his parents' bedroom, where he ran back and forth from one side of the bed to the other. "Time to get up! Time to get up! Pathways School! Pathways School!"

Mr. Green looked up at his bedside clock and flopped back down on the bed. "Jake, it's five o'clock in the morning. You don't need to get up yet."

"Yes…Pathways School!" Jake paced back and forth in front of his parents' bed.

Knowing that there was no winning, Mrs. Green got out of bed and walked over to him. Turning Jake to face her, she gently touched his hand. "Look at your cell phone, Jake. What time is it?"

"5:06 AM."

"That's right," Mrs. Green whispered. "And what time do we need to leave for school?"

7:30 AM."

"And how much time is that from now?" she asked.

"Two hours and 24 minutes."

"Good job, Jake," Mr. Green mumbled from under the covers. "You really are a math whiz."

"Yes, you are," his mom agreed. "But do you think it will take you that long to get ready for school?"

"No. 5 minutes to get dressed; 10 minutes to eat my cheerios, sliced banana, and milk; 3 minutes to brush my teeth; and 10 minutes of Jake chill time." Mrs. Green always made sure Jake had some time to relax before he left for school. "28 minutes in all!" Jake said proudly.

"Excellent, Jake. So, do you think you have some time to go back to bed and rest for a while? You have a big day ahead of you."

Jake closed his eyes and thought for a second. "Yes…1 hour, 56 minutes. Wake-up time…7:02 AM." Jake looked at his cell phone, reset his alarm, and ran back to bed. Mr. and Mrs. Green breathed a sigh of relief and went back to sleep until the next alarm awakened them for the first day of school.

❧

Three hours later, Leah had been dropped off at Royal Palm, and Jake and Jordie were settling into their fifth-grade classroom at Pathways. With backpack safely stored in his cubby, Jake walked over to his desk, where he found his name. Jake sat down, placed his homework planner and pencil case on his desk, and stared at the clock.

"*8:16 AM…8:16 AM…*," he whispered to himself. *Four more minutes.*

Jake knew that class began at 8:20. That's what their teacher Miss Davis (aka Miss D) had told them at student orientation. Jake was so absorbed with counting minutes that he did not seem to notice the other kids in the class. There were two other boys besides him and two other girls besides Jordie. He also didn't see that Jordie had dumped out everything from her brand new tie-dyed backpack on the floor.

"Miss D! Miss. D! My planner and pencil case…they're gone!" cried Jordie.

Before Miss D had a chance to respond, a really tall girl with short brown hair, bangs, brown eyes, and shiny blue glasses plopped down on the floor next to Jordie.

"Here they are," she said, handing Jordie's planner and pencil case to her.

"Where were they?" asked Jordie.

"Under your chair."

"What's your name?" asked Jordie.

"I'm Emily. What's yours?"

"Jordie. Thanks for helping me. I'm always losing things. My mom says if my head wasn't attached, I'd lose that, too."

"With my thick glasses, I can see everything," Emily said. "But don't worry about losing stuff. The teachers here always give us special backpack luggage tags. You'll never lose anything again."

"Luggage tags? Why?"

"They're not the kind of luggage tags you put on suitcases with your name and address. They look like luggage tags but have a list of stuff written on them to help you remember what to put in your backpack at school and home. Here's mine from last year." Emily lifted her backpack from the floor next to her desk.

"What a great idea!" said Jordie.

"We'd better put our backpacks in our cubbies," Emily said. "Class is gonna start. I'll help you put your stuff away."

When the bell rang at 8:20 AM, Jordie and Emily were seated at their desks. They were both in the front row, with

Jake in between them. With pencil in hand and planner on the corner of her desk, Jordie was ready and smiling ear to ear. Her brother seemed to be doing okay, and she had a new friend.

5

SOMETHING NEW

"Good morning, students! Welcome to fifth grade!"
"Good morning, Miss D!" the children responded.

"Miss Ross and I are so happy to see all of you! This year we have six wonderful students in our class. Four of you were with us in fourth grade, and two of you are new to Pathways. We can't wait to work together with all of you!"

"Although we have the same classroom from last year, there are lots of new things. So, look around, and see if you can spy something *new*. Use your eagle eyes to see what you can find. But…there are two rules. First, you have to keep silent until it's your turn, and second, you need to listen quietly while others are sharing. I'll go first."

Miss D walked around the room looking for something new. "I've got it!" she said. "I spy our two new students. Jordie and Jake Green. Let's welcome them with our silent rainbow cheer."

All the students except Jake and Jordie stood up and waved their arms to make a big arch above their heads. The kids loved silent cheers, since cheering aloud would disturb other classes during learning time.

31

"We're so glad to have the two of you in our class. Why don't you go next? But…since everything would be new to you, maybe you can pick something you find interesting. Jordie, you can go first."

Jordie thought for a second and then remembered Emily's backpack. "I know!" she exclaimed. "The luggage tag on Emily's backpack. Can me and Jake have one, too?"

"Excellent spying, Jordie! And yes, you and Jake will get a backpack tag. Everyone in the class will get a new one especially made for fifth grade. Let's move onto Jake. What interesting thing do you spy that stands out to you?"

Jake stood up, looked down, and pointed to his feet. "Something new! Air Jordan Basketball Shoes!" he declared. Jake then walked around the class to show all the kids his new shoes. Just as everyone started laughing, Miss D jumped in.

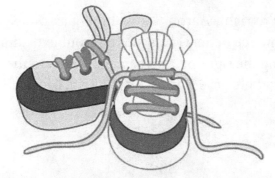

"Thank you, Jake. We can see you're very excited about your new shoes." Miss D guided Jake back to his seat. "Let's give Emily a turn now."

"I spy, I spy..." Emily's eyes wandered around the room. "I spy Ruthie. You cut your hair! It's so pretty!"

Ruthie scrunched down in her seat in the back row and put her hand on her chin. Although she loved her new short brown hair, Ruthie was shy and didn't like getting so much attention. Miss D knew how Ruthie felt and moved on quickly to the next student.

"What about you, Aaron? What do you spy that's new?"

"I spy your glasses. How come you have eyeglasses, Miss D?"

"You're right, Aaron. I now have glasses just like you to help me see better. I was having trouble reading books and seeing the signs on the road. So, I went to the eye doctor and got blue eye glasses, just like the color of Emily's."

Emily beamed. She couldn't believe that she and Miss D both had glasses the same exact color.

"Look at my glasses, Miss D," Aaron blurted out. "They're black...just like my hair." Aaron stood up, took off his glasses, and waved them around to show everyone.

"Yes, Aaron. Your glasses are a perfect match." Miss D smiled. "Okay, Noah, it's your turn. What do you spy that's new?"

"I spy the clock."

"That's not new!" Aaron shouted.

"You're right, Aaron," said Miss D, "but in this game, you only speak when it's your turn."

"Noah, can you tell us something new that you spy?"

"Something new?" Noah looked puzzled. With his finger on his chin and his thick, reddish-brown hair falling close to his right eye, he seemed confused. Noah had a hard time paying attention, so Miss D often needed to give him reminders to focus.

"Yes, Noah…tell us something new that you didn't see last year."

Noah looked around and suddenly his eyes hit on the wall next to the white board.

"I got it! The title on the front wall. It says *Our Fifth Grade Wall of Promises*. That's new."

"Good job, Noah!" praised Miss D.

"But what does it mean?" Aaron asked.

"Great question! But I can't answer it right now. We have a busy morning ahead. First, our welcome assembly…

next a school tour followed by recess…and then lunch. My secret will have to wait until this afternoon!" Miss D winked her eye and smiled. "Before we line up at the door, let's review our hallway rules. Who can share them with Jake and Jordie?"

Noah, Aaron, Emily, and Ruthie stood up immediately and responded in unison.

Zip your lips.
Stand up tall.
Hands by your side
In the hall.

"Excellent!" Miss D said. "Looks like we're ready." When she opened the door, all six students were in a straight line, and not a peep could be heard.

6

PROMISES

After a busy morning of activities followed by lunch, Miss D's fifth graders returned to their classroom. As they got settled in their seats, Jordie turned towards Emily. "I can't believe how big this school is! I hope Jake and I don't get lost."

"Don't worry, Jordie," said Emily. "You'll get used to it. "I'll help you."

"We'll all help you and Jake," Miss D said, reassuring them. "Wherever you go, you'll always have a buddy until you know your way."

"I know where to go!' Jake said confidently. "Out the door and 10 steps left to the bathroom…out the door, 50 steps down the hall to the exit sign, down the stairs 5 steps, turn right, and 30 steps to the playground…out the door, 50 steps down the hall to the exit sign, down the stairs 5 steps, turn right, and 100 steps to the cafeteria…."

"How do you know that?" asked Noah.

All the students were surprised.

"He's just making that up," Aaron snapped.

"Hold on, Aaron. You know we don't make accusations without knowing the facts," Miss D said, correcting him.

Aaron scrunched down into his seat and crossed his arms. "No way he's telling the truth!" he said, sneering.

Miss D ignored Aaron's behavior and continued talking. "When we were walking around, I noticed that Jake was counting his steps wherever we went."

"I saw him, too," said Emily. "Why were you doing that, Jake?"

Jake sat at his desk quietly and did not answer. It was as if he hadn't heard what Emily or anyone else had said. Jordie walked over to his desk, although she knew she wasn't supposed to leave her seat without permission.

"Jake always counts his steps," Jordie explained, as she put her hand on his shoulder to comfort him. "That way we never get lost!"

"You're so lucky, Jordie, to have such a helpful brother," said Miss D. "And we're so lucky to have you in our class, Jake. You'll be a great buddy to all of us!"

Jake looked up at Jordie and then Miss D. Feeling more comfortable, he turned towards Emily and the other kids. "Great buddy, Jake!" he exclaimed, feeling proud of himself.

"Everyone smiled, even Aaron.

"Okay fifth grade, let's get back to work. Time for my big secret!" Miss D walked over to the bulletin board. "This morning, Noah spied our *Fifth Grade Wall of Promises*, and Aaron asked what it meant. Can anyone guess?"

All the students sat quietly.

"Why would I create a wall that says *Fifth Grade Promises*?"

Miss D looked around to see if any of the students could answer her question.

Ruthie's hand inched up slowly. "Last year we had classroom *rules*. I think *Promises* is a better word," Ruthie whispered.

Miss D smiled and walked over to Ruthie. "You're absolutely right, Ruthie. Can you tell us why you think *promises* is a better word?"

"Rules are easier to break than promises," she said shyly.

"Like when we call out of turn," said Aaron. "That was a rule we broke lots of times last year."

"You're breaking it right now!" exclaimed Noah.

"Am not! We don't have any rules yet," Aaron retorted.

"Let's settle down, boys," Miss D said. "Calling out was one of our rules, but let's get back to what Ruthie said. Why are rules easier to break than promises?"

Emily raised her hand.

"I know, Miss D. A rule is something we have to obey because you say so. A promise is something we want to do."

Jordie's hand shot up.

"Go on, Jordie. Tell us what you think."

"A promise comes from your heart. When you're about to make a promise, my mom says you need to think about it a lot because people will be counting on you to do what you said you would do. If you break your promise, you hurt someone and that makes you feel bad, too."

"Emily and Jordie are both right," Miss D responded. "A promise is something we choose to do. So what kind of promises do you think fifth grade should make this year?"

Jake stood up and began to pound his fist on his chest. "Promises to put in our heart! Promises for our heart!'

"Yes, Jake! We need to make a list of promises that I can count on all of you to keep because you want to keep them. So, let's look back at our 10 fourth grade rules." Miss D turned on her computer and projected the rules on the classroom Smartboard. "Let's take a vote and pick 5 out of these 10 rules, which you feel in your heart that you can promise to follow."

"Put in the one about raising your hand and not calling out," Aaron blurted out.

"Good choice," said Miss D. Although Aaron had just called out, she chose to ignore his outburst. "I'm sure you'll work very hard to keep this promise once we finish our list. Right, Aaron?"

"Right, Miss D!"

Emily and Jordie's hands shot up.

"Can we do the one about respect?" asked Emily. "My mom says being respectful is really important."

"And I like the one about being ready with all your stuff when your class begins," said Jordie. I have a hard time with that."

"What about paying attention?" asked Noah. "That's hard for me."

Last was Ruthie. "Would the one about doing our homework and classwork be okay?" she asked meekly.

"More than okay!" Miss D exclaimed. "I think we have our list. Let's call it our *Fifth Grade Promises Pledge*!"

For the rest of the afternoon, the grade five students worked together on their wall of promises. In addition to their *Promises Pledge*, a tally chart was created on which Miss D would put hearts when she noticed students keeping their promises. Students also made their own charts so they could tally all the times they thought they were keeping promises. Finally, they came up with rewards that could be earned when they followed through on their promises.

As Miss D and Miss Ross's fifth grade class got ready for the bell to ring at 3:30 PM, all six students smiled with satisfaction. With their backpacks organized and zipped up, no one was happier than Jordie. Her new fifth grade laminated backpack tag was checked in all the right places. For the very first time, she felt confident that she had everything she would need for her first night after the very first day of school.

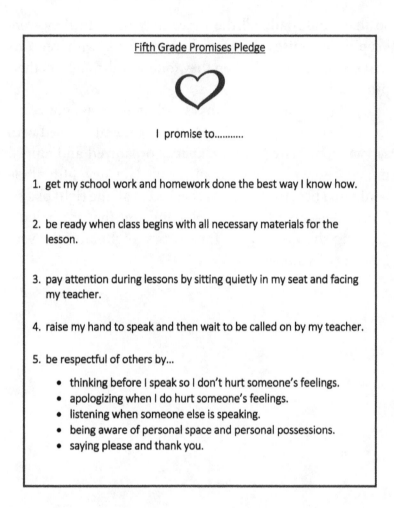

Fifth Grade Promises Pledge

I promise to...........

1. get my school work and homework done the best way I know how.

2. be ready when class begins with all necessary materials for the lesson.

3. pay attention during lessons by sitting quietly in my seat and facing my teacher.

4. raise my hand to speak and then wait to be called on by my teacher.

5. be respectful of others by...

   - thinking before I speak so I don't hurt someone's feelings.
   - apologizing when I do hurt someone's feelings.
   - listening when someone else is speaking.
   - being aware of personal space and personal possessions.
   - saying please and thank you.

ANYTHING IS POSSIBLE!

Our Promises Pledge Tally Chart

I Promise to......	Aaron	Emily	Jake	Jordie	Noah	Ruthie
get my school work and homework done the best way I know how.						
be ready when class begins with all necessary materials for the lesson.						
pay attention during lessons by sitting quietly in my seat and facing my teacher.						
raise my hand to speak and then wait to be called on by my teacher.						
be respectful of others by: ✓ thinking before I speak so I don't hurt someone's feelings. ✓ apologizing when I do hurt someone's feelings. ✓ listening when someone else is speaking. ✓ being aware of personal space and personal possessions. ✓ saying please and thank you.						

Rewards For Keeping Our Promises

Individual Rewards	Class Rewards
♦ 5 minutes Chillax time	♦ Special snack or treat
♦ iPad time	♦ Ice cream party
♦ Use of the teacher's chair	♦ Movie Day
♦ Good job phone call home	♦ Order in lunch
♦ Extra money for class store	♦ Extra recess

7

CHILL TIME

At 4:30 PM, Brayden, Jason, Rebecca, and Maddie arrived home from Royal Palm Academy, along with new neighbor Leah. Grabbing their backpacks, they piled out of the Hoffman's minivan at exactly the same time as Mrs. Green pulled into her driveway with Jordie and Jake.

"Mom!" shouted Leah.

Hearing his younger sister's voice as he got out of the car, Jake dropped his backpack on the ground, picked up his basketball from the bushes by the driveway, and ran across the street to the Hoffman's house.

"Jason! Brayden!" Jake yelled. "21! 21!"

"No, Jake!" Jordie said, running after him. "Mom said no basketball now."

"21! 21!" Jake repeated, as he threw his ball to Jason.

"Hey, Jake. Wish we could play, but we can't."

"School rules," Brayden said, with a big frown. "No sports, TV, or video games until homework is done."

Jake continued shouting and started spinning in circles. Seeing that Jake was getting out of control, Mrs. Green rushed across the street.

"Jake," said Mrs. Green. "I know how much you want to play with the boys, but they have homework."

Jake ignored his mother and began to swing his arms wildly. He was now in a full-blown tantrum. Brayden, Jason, Rebecca, and Maddie did not know what to do. Seeing the looks on her children's faces, Mrs. Hoffman walked over to Jake.

"Jake," she whispered. "If it's okay with your mom, you and the boys can play ball for ten minutes. We can use the timer on your watch. When the alarm rings, the game is over. And then you, Jordie, and Leah can join us for a snack. I brought home special cupcakes to celebrate the first day of school."

Mrs. Green didn't answer right away. She just wasn't sure that giving in to Jake was the right thing to do. *Why should he get a reward for bad behavior?* she thought to herself. But then she looked at all her children—Jake, Jordie, and her younger daughter Leah. This was a hard time for all of them. They had just come to a new neighborhood and a new school where they had to make new friends. Change was hard and was especially hard for Jake.

"Yes, it's okay," she said, turning towards Jake and Mrs. Hoffman. "But just for today."

Suddenly, Jake got silent. He stopped spinning, and his arms fell to his sides. His mother walked closer and spoke to him in a low, soothing voice. She knew how difficult it was for Jake to focus after one of his tantrums.

"Jake, did you hear what we said?"

Jake did not respond. Mrs. Green put her hands gently on Jake's shoulders and continued to speak. "You can have ten minutes of basketball, a cupcake, and then we go home. But next time, homework before basketball. Those are the rules."

Jake turned towards Mrs. Hoffman. "Ten minutes of basketball.... How many minutes for a snack?" he asked.

"Well...since it's still early, I think we can extend snack time a bit," she answered. "How about thirty minutes, so all you kids can have a chance to talk about your first day of school?"

Mrs. Green nodded her head in agreement.

Jake thought for a few seconds, looked down at his watch, and then closed his eyes. Finally opening them, he responded. "Ten minutes of basketball...thirty minutes for snack and talk...forty minutes in all. Home at 5:20 PM. Next time, school rules."

"Game on! 5:20 it is!" Jason shouted.

While the boys played their allotted ten minutes of basketball, the four girls raced inside to the kitchen to get their first pick of the cupcakes. In what seemed like seconds, Maddie and Leah were done and went upstairs to Maddie's room. Rebecca and Jordie were still at the kitchen table.

"Hurry up, Jordie!" said Rebecca.

"This cupcake is so good!" Jordie exclaimed. "I wish it would last forever."

"You gotta finish it now. I have something I have to show you," Rebecca insisted.

"What is it? Tell me now!"

"You'll see," Rebecca said, with a gleam in her eye.

Jordie took one last bite, licked her fingers, and then followed Rebecca upstairs.

"Close your eyes," Rebecca said, while opening her bedroom door. Taking Jordie by the hand, she led her into her room and made her sit down on her bed. "Don't peek!"

"I'm not peeking!" Jordie said, laughing. "Show me already!"

Rebecca went into her closet and took out the happy word painting she had made for her. "Okay," she said. "Now stand up and get on your toes!"

Jordie's eyes popped wide open. "I can't believe it! You made my *On My Toes* painting. I love it!"

Just like Rebecca promised, the painting had pink sparkly ballet slippers with stars all around them.

On My Toes!

"I've gotta show this to my mom," said Jordie. Grabbing the painting, Jordie ran downstairs. "Mom! Mom!" she shouted. "You gotta see what Rebecca made for me."

Jordie ran through the kitchen where Jake, Brayden, and Jason were eating cupcakes.

"Wait, Jordie," Jason mumbled, as chocolate drooled down his chin. "We want to see, too."

But she did not stop.

"Mom! Mom! Where are you?"

"Wait up, Jordie!" shouted Rebecca. "I know where she went…my mom's office. I'll show you."

With Rebecca in the lead, Jordie followed with Jason, Brayden, and Jake trailing behind. Maddie and Leah, who had heard all the shouting, were now there, too. Everyone wanted to see what Jordie had in her hand. Before they could get very far, Mrs. Hoffman and Mrs. Green appeared.

"Whoa!" said Mrs. Green. "Everyone freeze! Why are you shouting, Jordie?"

49

"Look, Mom. Look at what Rebecca made for me." Holding her *On My Toes* painting above her head so everyone could see, Jordie was smiling from ear to ear. So was Rebecca.

"That's beautiful, Rebecca!" exclaimed Mrs. Green. "What do the words mean, Jordie?"

"These are my *happy words* that make me feel good. Whenever I feel bad, I can look at them. They'll remind me that I can achieve anything. When I stand on my toes, like I do in ballet class, I can reach for the stars! Rebecca has a happy word, too. Tell them, Rebecca."

"My word is *different.* Everyone is different, and that's a good thing. When I look at my happy word painting, it reminds me that I have my own special talents, like painting."

"I want a happy word!" demanded Jake.

"I'll make you a happy word painting," said Rebecca. "What should I paint?"

Jake closed his eyes again and began to think. After a few seconds, he had his idea.

"*Chill time,*" Jake said. "I want *Chill time.*"

"What does that mean?" asked Brayden.

Since Jake had a hard time explaining things, Mrs. Green answered for him. "Jake is happiest when he feels calm. So, we have *Jake chill time* to help him relax."

"And Mom lets him hold his basketball," Leah added. "It really helps!"

Jake nodded and smiled at Leah.

"So that's what I'll paint," said Rebecca. "The words *Chill Time* with lots of basketballs around it."

"Yes!" exclaimed Jake. "Chill time with basketballs."

"What about me, Rebecca?" asked Maddie. "I want a happy word painting, too."

"Me, too," Leah said.

Rebecca couldn't believe all the attention she was getting. It felt so good to be *different* and to have a talent that her siblings and new friends did not have. "I'll do Jake first and then Maddie and Leah. Just let me know what happy words you want." Rebecca paused and then turned to her brothers. "What about you guys? Do you want happy word paintings?"

Brayden and Jason really wanted to say yes but were too embarrassed to admit it.

"Maybe," Jason said. "Brayden and me will get back to you."

"No biggie," Rebecca replied. "I have plenty of takers."

"5:20 PM. Time to go home," Jake declared.

"Yes, Jake, it's time to go home," said Mrs. Green. "Say goodbye and thank you to the Hoffmans."

"Goodbye and thank you to the Hoffmans," Jake repeated. As he walked out the door with his basketball in hand, Brayden and Jason each gave him an *Air High Five*. Leah hugged Maddie. Jordie hugged Rebecca. And even their moms hugged each other. The Hoffmans and Greens were on their way to becoming the best of friends.

8

BACKPACK PATROL

On the second day of school, Jake was ready and waiting by the door with backpack in hand at 7:28 AM. At 7:30, so were Mom, Jordie, and Leah. They knew that leaving for school on time was very important to Jake.

"Let's go," said Mrs. Green. "First stop, Royal Palm and then onto Pathways."

The kids piled into Mom's SUV. While Jake stared out the window and seemed to be lost in thought, Jordie was busy reviewing her new backpack luggage tag. Although there were checkmarks next to everything she needed to bring to school, she wasn't sure she had done it right.

"Why can't I ever remember where I put my stuff?" Jordie mumbled.

"Homework planner—inside zipper...homework folder—backpack center...pencil case—outside pocket," replied Jake.

Jordie quickly unzipped her bag and found her supplies.

"Thanks, Jake. How did you know where they were?"

"Jake knows all that kind of stuff," said Leah. "But what about the paper you asked Mom to sign last night? Do you have that?"

"Our Fifth Grade Promises Pledge!' Jordie exclaimed. "Mom, you gotta turn around. I don't have it."

Jake looked at his watch. "Too late…7:40 AM…time for school."

"No!" shouted Jordie. "I can't go to school without it. We have to go back!"

"Calm down, Jordie," Mrs. Green said softly. "I have your Promises Pledge. You and I signed it last night, but you forgot to put it in your bag." Mrs. Green stretched her arm over the back of her seat and handed Jordie the paper. "Put it in your homework folder right now so you don't forget it."

"Thanks, Mom! I promise. I won't forget anything ever again."

"Glad to hear that, Jordie," Mrs. Green said, chuckling. "But I think you might need some help from the Green team."

"Green Team? What's that?" asked Leah.

"That's us…our family," said Mom. "We can help Jordie."

"Backpack Patrol!" Jake shouted. "We need Backpack Patrol!"

"Backpack Patrol," Mom repeated. "What do you think, Jordie?"

Jordie didn't answer right away. Although she wished she could organize all her supplies by herself, she thought it would be easier if she had some help. Mom always said that was what families were for—to be there for each other whenever one of them had a problem.

"I'm in," she said. "But only if Jake is the leader. He knows where everything is."

"Backpack Patrol Leader!" her brother shouted, with a big smile on his face.

"Okay," agreed Mom. "Sounds like we have a plan."

Mrs. Green pulled into Royal Palm. When they reached the front of the carpool line, Leah opened the door. Just as she was about to exit, she turned back towards her brother and sister. "See you later, Green Team!" She giggled, then slammed the door and ran into school.

It was now 7:50 AM. Until they reached Pathways, the words *Backpack Patrol Leader* echoed throughout the car. Neither Mom nor Jordie seemed to mind. Jake would be a perfect Backpack Patrol Leader, and that was just what the Green family needed.

❧

At 8:05 AM, Jake and Jordie walked into their classroom. "We're here, Miss D," Jordie announced.

"Good morning, Jordie. Good morning, Jake. Please put your backpacks in your cubbies and get ready for class."

"Hey, Jordie!" shouted Emily. "Me and Ruthie are back here."

Forgetting Miss D's instructions, Jordie dumped her backpack on the floor next to her desk and went to the back table to join the girls. While the three girls chatted, Jake stashed his belongings in his cubby and went to his desk. It was 8:10 AM, and Jake wanted to be ready when the bell rang for class to begin.

Just as he was about to sit down with his homework planner, pencil case, and promises pledge in hand, the words *Backpack Patrol* popped into his head. Jake dropped his supplies on his desk. He grabbed Jordie's backpack and raced to the back of the room.

"Hey, what are you doing with my backpack?" Jordie said, sounding irritated.

"Backpack Patrol!" Jake yelled.

Jordie stood up. Not wanting Emily and Ruthie to know anything about the Green Team or Backpack Patrol, she tried to move away from the table. "That's for home, Jake. Not school," she whispered.

"Backpack Patrol," Jake shouted into Jordie's face.

"What's backpack patrol?" asked Emily.

"It's nothing," Jordie mumbled. "'I have to put my stuff away."

Just as Jordie tried to pull her bag from Jake, he tightened his grip.

"Jake, stop it!" Jordie screamed. "Give me my bag. Miss D! Miss Ross!"

"Backpack Patrol!" Jake repeated and started spinning.

"Jake...Jordie," called Miss D. "What's going on?"

"Jake took my backpack. Tell him to give it to me!"

Miss D put her arm around Jordie and looked directly at Jake. "Let's take five," she said in a soothing voice. "Miss Ross, would you take over the class for a few minutes. Jordie, Jake, and I need some private time. Why don't the three of us go outside and sit on the bench near the basketball court?"

Suddenly, Jake got silent, stopped spinning, and dropped Jordie's backpack. Miss Ross and all the other fifth grade students stared in surprise. They were amazed that Miss D had gotten Jake to calm down so fast. But

Jordie wasn't surprised. Like Miss D, she knew that Jake loved basketball. It was almost as if the word *basketball* had magical power.

Miss D picked up Jordie's backpack and walked the twins outside. When they got to the basketball court, she sat down on the bench and directed Jake and Jordie to sit on each side of her. She then turned towards Jordie.

"Can you tell me what happened this morning?"

Jordie nodded her head and tried to speak, but all that came out were sobs and tears. Miss D put her arm around her shoulders and tried to comfort her.

"It's okay to cry, Jordie. Crying is a good thing. It gets rid of all those angry feelings we sometimes have inside of us."

Within minutes, her tears subsided.

"Now take a deep breath, and tell me what happened."

"It all started in the car. I couldn't remember if I had put all my stuff in my bag. But Jake knew and told me where I put everything. Then I couldn't find my Promises Pledge. When I started freaking out, Mom said she had it. I was so happy and promised I would never forget anything ever again. Mom didn't think I could do that without help. That's when Jake shouted *Backpack Patrol*. We all decided that we should have a Green Team Backpack Patrol to make sure we have all our stuff every day. I said that Jake should be our patrol leader cuz he's so good at knowing where things are. But this was supposed to be for home, not school. When Jake brought me my backpack and started shouting at me, I got so embarrassed. I didn't want Emily and Ruthie to see him helping me. If I listened to you, Miss D, this never would've happened. I'm sorry I didn't put my stuff away when you told me."

Jordie finished and was totally out of breath. She put her head down and covered her eyes with her hands.

"It's going to be okay, Jordie," Miss D said, trying to comfort her. "I'm very proud of you. Do you know why?"

Jordie looked up at Miss D. "Cuz I said I'm sorry?"

"Yes, I am happy you apologized for not following the directions I gave you, but there's something else."

Jordie sat quietly, trying to think what she had done to make Miss D proud of her. She couldn't come up with anything.

"What did you tell me about your feelings?" hinted Miss D.

"That I was happy that Mom had my Promises Pledge and…that I was embarrassed when Jake started shouting about Backpack Patrol."

"You got it, Jordie. I'm proud of you because you were able to express how you were feeling. So, let's talk about being embarrassed. Tell me why you felt that way."

"Cuz I didn't want anybody to know that I needed Jake to help me organize my backpack. They'd think I was a baby and probably laugh at me."

"Let's go back to what happened in the car. Whose idea was it to make Jake Backpack Patrol Leader?" asked Miss D.

"Mine," Jordie said. "Jake's so good at finding things and putting them away in the right places."

"Good for you, Jake," Miss D said, turning towards him. "I'm so glad you're in my class. I think all of us in fifth grade can use your help—even Miss Ross and me."

Hearing Miss D's words, Jake smiled.

Jordie couldn't believe what she was hearing. Miss D wanted Jake's help. *Amazing!* she thought to herself. Suddenly, an idea popped into her head.

"Miss D, do you think we could have a Backpack Patrol in our class like we're gonna have at home?"

"I think that's a splendid idea. What do you think, Jake?"

"Grade 5 Backpack Patrol!" he shouted.

"I should've thought about that idea when we came to class this morning," said Jordie.

"How do you think that would that have changed what happened?" asked Miss D.

Jordie closed her eyes and tried to remember everything that happened when Jake brought her bag to the back of the room. *If I hadn't yelled at Jake,* she thought to herself, *I could have....*

"I know! When Jake brought me my backpack, I should have told Emily and Ruthie about Backpack Patrol. They would've thought it was a good idea. Even you said that it's *splendid.*"

"Yes, I did," Miss D said, chuckling. "It *is* splendid."

"I guess it was silly that I felt embarrassed," whispered Jordie.

"Feelings are never silly," Miss D said, reassuring her. "Everyone has feelings. The important thing is how we deal with them. And right now, you're doing an excellent job figuring out why you felt embarrassed and how you can feel better. Good job, Jordie! I'm proud of you."

Miss D turned back to Jake. "I'm also proud of you, Jake. You have wonderful organizational skills that will help your family and your classmates, too. But...we need to talk about the best way you can share your special skills. Do you remember the list of five promises we made yesterday?"

Jake nodded.

"Let's talk about the fifth one—"

"Respect!" interrupted Jake. "Thinking before I speak so I don't hurt someone's feelings, apologizing when I do hurt someone's feelings—"

"That's okay, Jake. You don't need to recite them all."

But Jake continued until he was finished.

"—listening when someone else is speaking, being aware of personal space and personal possessions, saying please and thank you."

"Excellent, Jake. You have a wonderful memory. So, let's talk about being respectful by being aware of personal space and personal possessions. Why do you think we should talk about that one?"

"I know!" exclaimed Jordie.

"Good, Jordie, but I asked Jake. Why should we talk about personal space and possessions?"

Jake closed his eyes. Both Miss D and Jordie knew he was thinking.

"Jordie's backpack," he said. "Jordie's personal posses-sion. I took it."

"Good job, Jake!" praised Miss D. "And what about personal space?"

Jake stared at Jordie. "Jordie's face. I shouted in Jordie's face."

"That's right, Jake. When you took Jordie's backpack and shouted in her face, you did not show respect for her personal possession or space. Do you think you can honor that promise in the future?"

Jake stood up and walked closer to Jordie, but not too close. He picked up her backpack and handed it to her gently. "Homework planner—inside zipper…pencil case—outside pocket…Promises Pledge—homework folder…I am respectful Jake," he said, while tapping his pointer finger on his chest.

"Well done, Jake. Now I know why your family chose you as their Backpack Patrol Leader. In fact, I think you will be my first choice for our Grade 5 Backpack Patrol Leader when we begin our weekly job chart. High Fives for Jake and Jordie!" exclaimed Miss D.

Just as Miss D, Jake, and Jordie began to walk back to their classroom, the bell rang.

"8:20 AM!" yelled Jake. "Time for class."

"Time for class," Miss D and Jordie echoed. They all were ready for the second day of school.

9

PROMISES PLEDGE # 4

"Good morning, fifth grade! So nice to see everyone in their seats ready with their homework and supplies."

"Miss D, when do we get to fill in our tally charts?" Aaron called out.

"Very soon, Aaron. But first we need do a quick review of all the promises we made yesterday." Miss D walked over to the bulletin board where the Grade 5 Promises were posted and called on students to read them aloud. When they were done, she pointed to the fourth promise on the list. "Emily, will you read Number 4 again?"

Emily adjusted her shiny blue glasses so she could see the board clearly. "*I promise to raise my hand to speak and then wait to be called on by my teacher.*"

"Thank you, Emily. Class, how do you think we're doing so far with honoring this promise?"

"Not so good," answered Emily. "I raised my hand before but didn't wait for you to call on me."

"You just called out again and didn't raise your hand!" Aaron shouted.

"So did you, Aaron!" snapped Jordie.

All the kids turned towards Aaron and started laughing.

"Freeze, Grade 5!" ordered Miss D. Everyone immediately became silent and didn't move.

"Now…I want everyone to take a deep breath and focus your attention on me." Miss D then turned to Emily. "I bet it was hard for you to admit that you didn't wait for me to call on you. Good for you!"

Emily smiled.

"But Emily isn't the only one in our class who has had trouble with Promise Number 4. Everyone seems to have forgotten this promise. Why did we all decide yesterday that raising your hand and then waiting to be called on are important?"

Everyone's hand shot up.

"Jordie, I saw your hand first and then Ruthie's and Noah's. Go ahead, Jordie."

"It's like what happened today, Miss D. None of us raised our hands, and we all started calling out. It got crazy, and you had to say *freeze*."

"That's right, Jordie. Ruthie, you're next."

"Calling out is bad manners," she whispered. "We need to be respectful just like it says in our fifth promise."

"Excellent, Ruthie. What about you, Noah?"

"Calling out is unfair."

"Why do you think it's unfair, Noah?"

"If I'm talking and someone calls out, it interrupts me. Then I forget what I was gonna say. I don't like when that happens. I get so confused."

"You're right, Noah. Everyone gets confused when their thoughts get interrupted. How many of you feel confused or frustrated when someone shouts out and interrupts what you're saying?"

Miss D looked around the class. Everyone's hand was up. "So how can we solve this problem? Jake?"

"Promise Number 4!" Jake opened his eyes as wide as he could, put his right hand on his heart, and said, *"I promise to raise my hand to speak and then wait to be called on by my teacher."*

"Good, Jake. Can the rest of you make the same promise?"

Following Jake's lead, Jordie, Emily, Ruthie, Noah, and Aaron stood up, put their hands on their hearts, and echoed Jake's words.

"Go, fifth grade!" cheered Miss D. "Now, let's do our tally charts."

While Miss D gave everyone a heart on the classroom chart for being ready with homework and supplies, the students filled in their own charts. When they were finished, all of them put their charts carefully inside their Promises folder.

"I wonder how many more promises you can keep this week?" said Miss D, winking her eye. "Time for writing!"

10

FREE TO BE ME

Writing! Jordie mumbled to herself. *I'm so bad at writing.* Jordie's face turned red—almost as red as her headful of curly red hair.

"Me, too," whispered Emily.

Jordie turned towards Emily. She hadn't realized that anyone could hear what she was saying. But Emily wasn't the only one who heard her. So did Miss D, but she acted as if she had not heard a sound. She looked around the room at all of her students and could tell that it wasn't just Jordie and Emily who looked unhappy. Miss D thought for a minute and then walked over to Miss Ross.

"Miss Ross, how do you feel about writing?"

Miss Ross answered immediately. "I love to write now, but when I was a student, like you guys, I didn't like to write at all."

"Why?' Miss D asked.

"I think it's because I could never think about what to write. And even when the teacher gave us a topic, I could never find the right words. What about you, Miss D?"

"I like to write now, too. But when I was a kid, spelling was very hard. I got so stuck on figuring out how to spell the words that I'd forget what I was going to write. I used to get really angry at myself… How about you, fifth grade? How do you feel about writing? Jordie?"

"Just like you felt, Miss D. My spelling is bad, too, but so is my reading. Even when I get help with spelling, sometimes I can't read what I write."

"That must be frustrating for you, Jordie. What about you, Emily?"

"I feel just like Jordie. I have dyslexia, so reading and writing are hard for me."

Jordie's eyes popped open. She couldn't believe that Emily had dyslexia, too.

"Who else would like to share their feelings about writing? Noah?"

"I read and spell okay, but when I write, I get distracted. I start writing a sentence and then forget what I was gonna say. My ideas get all jumbled up."

"Thanks for sharing your feelings, Noah. Ruthie, your turn."

"I like to write, but I don't want anyone to see it. I hate when I make mistakes. It makes me feel bad." Ruthie pulled down on her brown bangs, but they were really too short to hide her face.

"People often feel bad when they make mistakes," said Miss D. "But mistakes don't have to be a bad thing. They can actually be something good. We'll talk more about mistakes at another time. What about you, Jake?"

"I like writing lists...lots of lists...no stories...just lists."

"Great, Jake. I'm glad you mentioned lists. You might not like to write stories, but did you know that the very best writers often make lists of their ideas? They do that so they don't forget all the details they might want to include when they start writing their stories."

Jake didn't respond, but everyone could tell he was thinking about what Miss D said because he had his eyes closed.

Aaron was the last to go. With his hand waving back and forth, Miss D called on him.

"I hate writing!"

"Can you tell us why you don't like writing?"

"I just hate it!" Aaron threw his glasses down on his desk and crossed his arms across his chest. With a frown on his face, he turned away and refused to say anything more. Miss D didn't respond. She knew that it was best to talk with Aaron when he calmed down.

"So, it sounds like you all have some unhappy feelings about writing," said Miss D. "Just like Miss Ross and me when we were your age. Why do you like writing now, Miss Ross?"

"When I write, I feel free!"

Suddenly, Aaron turned back around. Putting his glasses on, he looked directly at Miss Ross and raised his hand. Miss Ross smiled and called on him.

"Miss Ross, why does writing make you feel free?"

Miss Ross walked over to Aaron. "When I write, I get to express all my feelings. Writing them down on paper makes me feel free. That's why I started writing a journal. It's so much fun!"

"I want to feel free!" Aaron exclaimed. "Miss D, can we write journals like Miss Ross?"

"That's a wonderful idea, Aaron. You took the words right out of my mouth," she said, chuckling. "We'll be talking about journal writing today."

Aaron was no longer frowning. *Miss D and I had the same idea. I can't believe it!* he thought to himself.

Noah's hand popped up next. "Miss Ross…"

"Yes, Noah?"

"Do you still have a hard time finding the right words like you did when you were a kid?"

"Sometimes. But it doesn't bother me anymore because now I know why finding the right words is difficult. Did you know that even famous authors struggle with finding the right words?"

"No way!" Aaron called out.

"It's true!" exclaimed Miss Ross. Ignoring Aaron's outburst, she explained why. "Words are very powerful. That's why we must choose each one carefully when we speak and when we write."

"Authors are word detectives," added Miss D. "Just like detectives who solve crimes, writers are also detectives. They search and search until they find just the right words to make the sentences in their stories sound the best they can be."

All the girls couldn't wait to speak. Emily went first.

"I want to be a word detective and write a journal. That sounds like fun!"

"Me, too," added Jordie and Ruthie.

"What about you, Jake?" asked Miss D.

"Can I make lists in my journal?"

"Yes, indeed, Jake. Lists are fine." Miss D then walked over to the white board and started writing.

"Miss D!" Ruthie shouted. "I have an idea. I know I'm not supposed to call out, but you gotta hear it."

Miss D turned around and actually smiled at Ruthie. Even though she'd forgotten to raise her hand and called out, this was the first time Ruthie had spoken up and acted sure of herself.

"It's okay, Ruthie. We all would love to hear your idea."

"I have a good name for our journals. Can we call them *Free to Be Me*?"

"Great idea! That's actually a popular name. There are books and even a song with the title *Free to Be Me*. But maybe everyone wants to name their own journals. Let's go around the room and poll the class."

The polling didn't take long. The vote was unanimous.

"*Free to Be Me* it is," Miss D declared. "Any other ideas?"

Jordie raised her hand.

"Yes, Jordie."

"Maybe we can have a *Word Detective* page in our journals. We could make a list of all the special words we find. Then we wouldn't forget them…and they'd be spelled right so we wouldn't make mistakes."

"What do you think, class? Should we add a *Word Detective* page to our journals?"

71

No polling was needed this time. Everyone's hand shot up immediately.

"Wonderful!" she exclaimed. "And I have the perfect activity to help you start your *Free to Be Me* journal." Miss D turned on her computer and walked over to the Smartboard. Projected on the screen was the very first page of their journal.

☆ *Presenting....Fabulous Fifth Grader!* ☆

_____

My Photo

Words That Describe Me

_____   _____

_____   _____

"*Presenting...Fabulous Fifth Grader!*", Miss D announced. "First, write your name on the line under the stars. Next, you will all come up with four words to describe yourself. Write them on the four lines on the bottom of the page. While you're doing that, I'm going to take a photo of each of you. When they are ready, you will paste yours under the words *My Photo*. Okay, word detectives, let's brainstorm some words you might want to use."

Everyone participated. Although they couldn't wait to share their ideas, they all remembered to raise their hands and not call out. After the white board was totally filled with words, the students chose the four words they each liked best and completed page number 1 of their *Free to Be Me* journals. Miss D's *Fabulous Fifth Graders* were proud of themselves. Not only were they remembering their Promises pledges, but they were also on their way to becoming *fabulous* writers!

11

Friday Afternoon

The first week of school was over. When Friday arrived, the Hoffman and Green kids couldn't believe how quickly the days had passed. Although they all were happy with their new classes and teachers, they always looked forward to the weekend. They especially loved Fridays because school always ended an hour earlier.

Standing at the carpool line, Jake paced back and forth. He couldn't wait to get home because Brayden and Jason had invited him to play basketball. Jordie couldn't wait either. She had to get home to see Rebecca. When Mrs. Green pulled up, Jake and Jordie raced to the car and jumped in.

"21!" shouted Jake. "Home, Mom, home!"

"Hurry, Mom," begged Jordie. "Rebecca and I have lots of stuff to do. It's not fair that Leah gets to go home with her and Maddie. She's probably already there."

"No, she's not," said Mrs. Green. "I just spoke to Mrs. Hoffman. They'll be home in 20 minutes, just like us."

"I still wish I could carpool with them," she grumbled to herself. "It's not fair!" Jordie scrunched down in her seat and stared at her watch. 20 minutes seemed like 20 hours. When they finally arrived home, the Hoffmans were pulling in just as Mrs. Green had predicted.

Jake and Jordie jumped out of the car. While Jake grabbed his basketball, Jordie took her homework folder and ran to the edge of the driveway.

"21!" yelled Jake.

"Wait!" Mrs. Green shouted. "What about your backpacks?"

"Please, Mom," Jordie said. "Can you take them inside?"

"Sure." Mrs. Green smiled. "Just this time."

"Thanks," Jordie shouted. "Let's go, Jake!"

"Hey, Jordie," said Rebecca. "What's in the folder? "I have something I gotta show you."

"21!" Jake yelled again.

"Chill, Jake," Brayden said. "We're waiting for Jason. He'll be out in a second.

"*Chill!*" shouted Rebecca. "I almost forgot. I made your happy word painting, Jake. Let's go get it."

Forgetting all about "21," Jake dropped his basketball and followed Rebecca and Jordie. As he ran upstairs to Rebecca's room, all he could think about was his painting.

"Here it is," Rebecca said with pride. "Just like you wanted it. *Chill Time* with lots of basketballs around it."

Chill Time!

"Look, Jake!" exclaimed Jordie. "One basketball has a clock with a timer. You love stopwatches."

Jake grabbed his happy word painting and ran out of Rebecca's room, shouting at the top of his lungs. "Chill Time! Chill Time!" Jake raced downstairs and outside to the basketball court where the Hoffman boys were waiting. All the girls followed, even Mrs. Hoffman.

"Look!" Jake shouted. "Chill Time! Rebecca made me my happy word."

"Nice!" said Jason.

"Look, Brayden! Look at my happy word!"

"That's great, Jake. Now let's play basketball."

"Basketball!" echoed Jake. "21!" But then Jake looked at his painting. As much as he wanted to play ball, he didn't want to let go of his happy word. Jordie understood how Jake felt and walked over to him.

"I'll hold onto your happy word, Jake," she whispered. "I promise to keep it safe."

Jake gave Jordie the painting and picked up his basketball.

"Game on!" shouted Brayden.

While the boys played ball, the four girls went back inside.

"What about our happy words?" Maddie asked, as they all plopped down on the couch in the family room.

"What words do you want?" said Rebecca.

"I want a word that has to do with gymnastics," Leah replied.

"Me, too!" exclaimed Maddie. "I want *passion*!"

"Why *passion?*" asked Leah.

"Because gymnastics is my passion. I can't live without it. It makes me so happy."

"I can make a picture of a gymnast doing a split," said Rebecca. "Do you want that?"

"Yes," said Maddie. "I love splits, handsprings, cartwheels…any kind of tumbling. Maybe someday I'll get a *Perfect 10*!"

"What about you, Leah?" asked Rebecca.

"Well…my favorite thing in gymnastics is the vault. I just love flying over it. So, I want the word *vault*. My coach always says that vault means leap and that if we want to succeed, we must always be willing to take a big leap."

"*Vault* it is!" declared Rebecca. "And I can make a picture of a vault to go with your happy word."

"Perfect," said Leah. "And maybe someday I'll get a *Perfect 10*, too!"

Maddie grabbed Leah's hand, and the two girls ran upstairs. Jordie and Rebecca now had the whole couch to themselves. Turning towards Jordie, Rebecca remembered the folder she had in her hand.

"So, what's in the folder, Jordie?"

"Something really special. You know how we both have dyslexia and have a hard time with reading and writing?"

"Yeah…what about it?" asked Rebecca.

"Well, I'm not so scared of writing anymore."

"Why not?"

"In school this week, our teachers were telling us how hard writing was for them when they were kids. It made us feel so good to know that they felt like we do. Then Miss Ross told us that she really likes writing now. When we asked her why, she said that writing makes her feel free because she gets to write down all her feelings in a journal. And that makes her feel really good. So, we all decided we wanted to write a journal." Jordie took her journal out of her homework folder. "Look, Rebecca. It's called *Free to Be Me!*"

"Wow!" said Rebecca. "That's a great name."

"Yeah. My friend Ruthie thought of it. But I came up with a good idea, too…a *Word Detective* page where you keep a list of words you like. When you get stuck trying to find the right words to use in a story, you can check your list. The best part is that they'll all be spelled the right way, so we don't have to worry about making mistakes."

"I want to write a journal!" Rebecca declared. "And I already know what I'm gonna write first."

"What?" Jordie asked. "You gotta tell me!"

"Not until I'm done," Rebecca said, teasing her friend. "I promise to show you the next time you come over…."

"Jordie! Leah!" called Mrs. Hoffman. "Time to go home!"

"Can't you tell me now?" Jordie asked. "We won't see you until Sunday afternoon."

Saturday was family day for the Hoffmans and Greens, and homework was always done on Sunday morning.

"No, Jordie," Rebecca said, with a gleam in her eye. "See you Sunday. That's when *I'll be free to be me*!"

SUNDAY MORNING

The Hoffman kids never looked forward to Sunday mornings. That was the time when all homework had to be done. And if they didn't finish, Sunday morning rolled into Sunday afternoon. Brayden, Jason, Rebecca, and Maddie knew the family rule: *No fun until homework is done.*

For Brayden and Jason, homework had become a competition to see who could finish first. They called it the *Sunday Morning Homework Race.* Although they each wanted to be the first one done, they knew they had to do their work carefully. If Mom or Dad saw them rushing through their homework, they'd be back in their rooms doing it again.

"I'm done," shouted Jason. Running past Brayden's room, Jason gave him a "V" sign for "Victory" and then pounded down the stairway to the family room. Nothing was going to stop him from getting first dibs on the TV remote.

"It's only eleven o'clock," Brayden grumbled. "How'd he finish so fast?" Brayden sighed and went back to his math homework. *Only three more problems, and I'm done,* he thought to himself. When he finished the last problem, Maddie appeared in his doorway.

"Beat you, Brayden!" she bragged. "I guess you're third in the homework race today."

"You're not in the homework race," he yelled. "Just Jason and me!"

"Do you think I really want to be in your dumb homework race?" snapped Maddie. "Not!"

"Me neither!" shouted Rebecca, who was now standing in her doorway across from Brayden's room.

"You'd never win anyway," Brayden said, sneering.

Rebecca slammed her door and flopped on her bed. "It's not fair!" she said. "Brayden's right. I'd never win that stupid race." Rebecca sighed and returned to her desk to finish her writing homework. Picking up her pen to put the final touches on her assignment, her anger suddenly disappeared—all because of Jordie. If not for her, Rebecca never would have come up with an idea for her first writing assignment—a paragraph about herself. Mrs. Brown, her sixth-grade teacher, wanted to get to know each of her new students. All week long, Rebecca couldn't come up with anything until Jordie had brought over her *Free to Be Me* writing journal. That's when an idea finally popped into her head. *A paragraph about things that make me feel free to be me!* she had said to herself.

Now it was Sunday, and her paragraph was done as well as the first two pages of her journal. As much as she wanted to go downstairs and watch TV and play video games with Maddie and the boys, she had a more important job to complete. Rebecca had to finish Maddie and Leah's happy word paintings before the Hoffmans went over to the Green's house for a barbecue dinner at 6:00 PM. "A promise is a promise." She sighed and got to work.

When five o'clock rolled around, Rebecca couldn't believe how long she had been painting. It was a good thing her mother had brought her a peanut butter and jelly sandwich. She was so into her work that she had forgotten about lunch.

"Finished!" Rebecca stared proudly at her paintings and then back at her journal. "They're gonna love them!" she exclaimed. She then went to her closet and found a roll of brown packing paper. After gently wrapping each painting, she placed them in a big shopping bag, along with her journal, and ran downstairs. Rebecca couldn't wait to get to the Green's house. Racing past Brayden, Jason, and Maddie, she made a beeline for the front door.

"Hey, where are you going?" yelled Jason.

"And what's in the bag?" asked Brayden.

Rebecca didn't answer. No way was she gonna tell them. After her long afternoon of hard work, everyone would just have to wait for *the big reveal*.

Rebecca ran past Mom in the living room. "Going to see Jordie," she shouted and slammed the door.

"Where'd she go, Mom?" asked Maddie.

"To the Green's."

"Why so early?"

Mrs. Hoffman shrugged. She had no idea.

"If Rebecca's going, so am I," said Maddie. Maddie ran upstairs to get her American Girl doll and then went across the street to play with Leah.

❧

"Jordie! Leah! It's me," called Rebecca. She rang and rang the bell, but no one answered. Just as Rebecca was about to give up, Jordie and Leah sneaked up from behind.

"Boo!" shouted Jordie.

Rebecca shrieked. "Jordie!" she said. "You scared me!"

"Gotcha!" Jordie laughed.

"Where were you?" asked Rebecca.

"We were in the back helping Mom and Dad get ready for the barbecue."

"I have something I gotta show you, Jordie. Let's go inside."

"What about Maddie?" asked Leah. "Where is she?"

"Right here!" Maddie shouted, as she ran down the driveway to join the girls.

"Take Maddie to the backyard," Jordie told Leah. "Rebecca and I have things to do."

"What?" asked Leah.

"Not your business!" snapped Jordie.

"Who cares what they're doing. Let's go," said Maddie.

When Maddie and Leah left, Rebecca followed Jordie inside the house into the kitchen.

"Let's sit here," said Jordie, eyeing a big bowl of tortilla chips and guacamole. As Jordie took a handful of chips, Rebecca grabbed a napkin and handed it to her.

"Wipe your hands, Jordie. I gotta show you my journal." Rebecca opened it and read the first page aloud…

This journal is dedicated to my new friend, Jordie Green. Without her, I would never have started a "Free To Be Me Journal". Every time I write in my journal, I will think about Jordie. She will always be my BFF — Best Friend Forever!

"Wow, Rebecca!" exclaimed Jordie. "I can't believe you dedicated your journal to me!"

"Why not?" asked Rebecca. "If it weren't for you, there'd be no journal, and I would never have come up with an idea for my first writing assignment. I had to write a paragraph about me and had no idea what to write until you showed me your journal. There's more. Listen…"

*Let me introduce myself. My name is Rebecca Hoffman. My favorite thing to do in the whole wide world is art. If I had the time, I would paint or draw all day long. Second to art is waterskiing. Nothing is better than crossing the wakes on one ski. I finally did that this summer at Camp Mineola on Lake Winnipesaukee in New Hampshire. I can't wait to go back there next year. Painting, drawing, and waterskiing make me feel so good. They make me feel **free to be me!***

"You waterski?" said Jordie. "I do, too!"

"Another thing that's the same about us," said Rebecca. "Red curly hair, dyslexia, backpacks, and now water skiing!"

Twins!" they both exclaimed and started laughing.

"I smell barbecue," said Jordie. "Let's go!"

Rebecca closed her journal and gently placed it back in her shopping bag along with the happy word paintings.

"Hey!" said Jordie. "What else is in the bag?"

"My secret surprise," said Rebecca, placing her bag behind her back.

"But I'm your best friend," she said.

"Sorry, Jordie." Rebecca chuckled. "You'll just have to wait like everyone else. Let's go. I'm hungry!"

13

THE BARBECUE

"Get your burgers!" shouted Mr. Green. Jake was first in line, with Brayden and Jason right behind him. The boys filled up their plates with hamburgers smothered in ketchup, corn on the cob, pickles, chips, and one of Dr. Hoffman's homemade, gooey chocolate chip cookies. They then moved inside to the Green's screened-in porch. Since it was a hot August summer day, two large overhead fans were blowing at full force. A long wooden table had been set with bowls of guacamole and chips and two large pitchers of ice-cold lemonade.

Brayden grabbed a pitcher, filled up a cup, and downed it in one gulp. He then poured two more cups for Jason and Jake and refilled his own. Just as the boys sat down to eat, their sisters and parents joined them. Within minutes, every morsel of food was gone. While Mrs. Green refilled everyone's cups with lemonade, Rebecca reached for her bag under the table.

"Time for my surprise!" she declared.

"What surprise?" asked Brayden.

Rebecca pulled out the packages she had so carefully wrapped earlier that day.

89

"What's that?" said Jason.

"Guess!" replied Rebecca, with a twinkle in her eye.

Leah and Maddie looked at each other. Suddenly, they knew. "Our happy word paintings!" The girls jumped up and grabbed them from Rebecca. They could not rip off the paper fast enough.

"Look!" exclaimed Leah. "Mine says *Vault*.

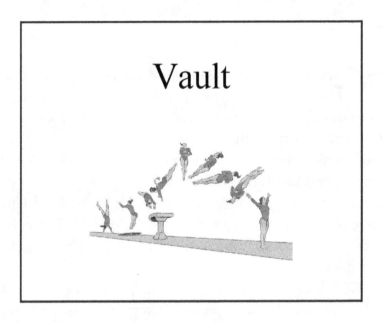

"Why *vault*?" asked Jason.

"*Vault* means leap," said Leah. "My coach says you always have to try to take big leaps if you want to win in gymnastics or in anything." Leah clutched her happy word painting to her chest. "This is the best!"

"Look at mine," Maddie yelled. "It says *passion* cuz gymnastics is my passion. That means I can't live without it! Thanks, Rebecca. I love it!"

Passion

"You really are talented!" exclaimed Mrs. Green.

Rebecca was beaming from ear to ear.

"Hey! What about our happy paintings?" asked Jason.

"You told me you'd get back to me when you and Brayden talked," replied Rebecca.

"We'll we've talked and know what we want. Right, Brayden?"

Brayden was clueless. He had no idea what kind of happy word painting he wanted. "You go first, Jason." Brayden needed time to think.

"I've got it," said Jason. "But it's three words, just like Jordie has." Jason paused. "Everybody ready?"

"Just say them!" Maddie said impatiently.

"On the ball!" exclaimed Jason. "It's a pun."

"What's a pun?" asked Leah.

"A pun is when you use a word in two different ways to make people laugh," Mrs. Hoffman explained.

"That's right," said Jason. "I love to play ball. That's one way to use the word. But when you say you're *on the ball,*

91

that means you are alert, quick, and ready to go. That's me! What about you, bro? What word do you want?"

Brayden was still thinking. *What word would make me feel happy?* he thought to himself. Nothing seemed to come to mind. Just as he was about to give up, he noticed the ketchup bottle still sitting in the middle of the table. "I've got it," he announced. "My happy word is *ketchup!*"

"*Ketchup?*" said Jordie. "Why'd you pick that word?"

Everyone in the Hoffman family was laughing. They all knew why. Brayden loved ketchup. He put ketchup on everything. He even ate ketchup all by itself!

"Ketchup is Brayden's *passion*," Jason said, glancing at Maddie. "He can never get enough ketchup. We call him the *Ketchup King.*"

"A ketchup bottle with crowns around it! That's what I'll paint," declared Rebecca.

Brayden smiled and then closed his eyes. He could see it now...his happy word painting on his wall staring down at him. Nothing would make him happier than a big bottle of ketchup.

Jake raised his cup of lemonade high in the air. "Here's to Happy Word Painter Rebecca!"

"To Happy Word Painter Rebecca," everyone shouted. And with this last toast of the evening, the Hoffmans went home. The weekend was over. There was lots to do before school the next day.

14

THE SECOND MONDAY

When the sun rose on Monday morning, there was no need for alarm clocks. The Hoffman and Green kids were already up. Even though the weekend was over, they all looked forward to going back to school. The second Monday of the school year was always the best. Unlike the very first day of school, when butterflies seemed to flutter in everyone's stomachs, the scary feelings disappeared in week number two. That was because students now knew their teachers and the kids in their classes. They were also becoming used to their weekly schedules and daily routines.

As Brayden, Rebecca, Jason, and Maddie got dressed, they could see the sun beginning to shine outside their bedroom windows. On the opposite side of the street, so could Jake, Jordie, and Leah. Although none of them said anything, they all had a look of contentment on their faces while they watched the sun move higher in the sky. It was almost as if the sun were smiling at them. It was going to be a very good day.

Jake and Jordie walked into class at exactly 8:00 AM. While Jordie got her supplies and put away her backpack in her cubby, Jake watched from afar. He remembered what Miss D had told him. *Don't take Jordie's backpack*, he thought to himself. *Don't shout in Jordie's face.*

Jordie could tell what Jake was thinking. She knew he was trying his best to respect her space and possessions. Walking past Jake, she whispered, "Backpack Patrol," and gave him a thumbs up. With a smile on his face, Jake went to sit down and looked at his watch. It was 8:05 AM—15 minutes before the bell for class to begin. While all the other kids were talking to each other, he opened his favorite book—*Stephen Curry: The Children's Book: The Boy Who Never Gave Up*. Jake loved to read this book over and over and over again. Steph Curry was his favorite basketball hero. Even though he had been too short to play basketball in high school, too weak to play in college, and not good enough to play in the NBA, Steph never gave up. He finally became an NBA All-Star!

Jake finished the final page and slammed the book shut just as the 8:20 AM bell rang. "I'll never give up!" he shouted.

"Glad to hear that, Jake," said Miss D, while the rest of the students got settled at their desks. "What a great attitude for the start of our second week of school. Even when something is hard to do, we should never give up. What do you think, class?"

Jake had his hand up first and stood up to show everyone the cover of his book. "Steph Curry never gave up!" he exclaimed. "I never give up."

"That's wonderful, Jake," replied Miss D. "But do you think you can use your *never give up* attitude in more than basketball?"

Jake did not answer. With his eyes closed, Miss D. could tell he was thinking.

"Do you need some more time?" she asked.

Jake nodded. Miss D. turned back to the class. "What do the rest of you think about not giving up?"

Noah and Aaron raised their hands.

"I love basketball!" exclaimed Noah.

"Me, too," agreed Aaron.

"Basketball is great," said Miss D. "But let's focus on the idea of not giving up in school when things get hard." Miss D went to the white board and began writing. When she was done, she turned back to the class. "Who can finish this sentence for me?"

When things get hard in school, I'll never give up on......

Emily and Jordie looked at each other and then raised their hands at the same exact time. Emily went first.

"When things get hard in school, I'll never give up on learning to read and write better even though I have dyslexia."

"Me, too!" declared Jordie, grabbing Emily's hand.

"Excellent, girls!" Miss D said. "I'm sure you both will make great improvements this year in both reading and writing."

Noah's hand shot up.

"Yes, Noah."

"I'll never give up on trying to pay attention. It's so hard, but I'll try to do better."

Miss D walked over to Noah and put her hand on his shoulder. "What an excellent promise. With your never give up attitude, I'm sure you'll succeed."

Ruthie and Aaron were next.

"I'll never give up on math," said Ruthie. "I just wish it was easier."

"I think Miss Ross and I can make it easier this year, Ruthie. We have a few new math tricks that will really help."

"Can you help me, too?" asked Aaron. "I hate math."

"Absolutely, Aaron," Miss D replied. "We have math tricks for you, too. In fact, Miss Ross and I spent part of our summer learning new ways to make math easier. That's because we never give up either!"

Aaron couldn't believe that his teachers were doing school work during their summer vacation, especially math. But if Miss D and Miss Ross weren't giving up on him, he could try harder.

"Okay, Miss D. I'll never give up on math!" he declared.

"Good for you, Aaron!"

Miss D then turned back to Jake. "Did you think of something else besides basketball?"

Jake stood up and pointed to the Fifth Grade Promises Pledge.

"I'll never give up on Pledge Number 5—*be respectful of others.*"

"Great choice, Jake," replied Miss D. "And since you brought up respect, that reminds me. We need to fill out our *Weekly Grade 5 Job Chart*. The first job assignment is for you, Jake. Since you are going to try really hard to be respectful of others, you will be our Backpack Patrol leader this week."

"Yes!" he shouted. "Respectful Jake. I'll never give up!"

Miss D smiled at Jake. She then unrolled the job chart and tacked it up on the bulletin board. "Now, let's get to the rest of our jobs. It's almost time for PE."

Miss D read aloud the list of jobs and explained each one. In addition to Backpack Patrol Leader, there was a Whiteboard Manager, a Door and Lights Monitor, a Materials Manager, a Pencil Sharpener, and a Snack Supervisor. When everyone was given a job and understood what was expected, Noah stood up and moved towards the door.

"Door and Light Monitor ready, Miss D. Time for PE," he announced.

"Good job, Noah!" exclaimed Miss D. "Looks like that *Never Give Up* attitude is working already."

Noah beamed. It felt really good to know that Miss D was proud of him. And now he was going to PE, where the fifth-grade boys were going to play basketball. Nothing could make him feel better than that!

Grade 5 Weekly Job Chart

Helper	Job	What I Need to Do
Jake	Backpack Patrol Leader	✓ In the morning, check that all students put away their backpacks and bring their homework folders and pencil cases to their desks. ✓ In the afternoon, check that all students put their pencil case, homework folder and assigned books into their backpacks to take home.
Ruthie	White Board Manager	✓ Change the date on the whiteboard each day. ✓ Write the homework on the whiteboard each day. ✓ Erase the whiteboard at the end of the day.
Noah	Door and Lights Monitor	✓ Hold the door when teachers and students enter and exit classroom. ✓ Turn on and off lights when teachers and students enter and exit classroom.
Emily	Materials Manager	✓ Pass out paper, worksheets, and any other materials needed for a lesson. ✓ Pass out supplies such as pencils, pens, markers, scissors, glue, etc.
Aaron	Pencil Sharpener	✓ At the end of each day, check all classroom pencils. ✓ Sharpen only pencils that need sharpening.
Jordie	Snack Supervisor	✓ Hand out snack. ✓ Supervise snack clean-up making sure desks are clear and garbage is thrown in trash basket.

15

THE SECOND MONDAY
(PART 2)

While Jake and Jordie were enjoying PE, Leah, Maddie, Brayden, Jason, and Rebecca were beginning their day at Royal Palm Academy. For Brayden and Jason, that meant seventh-grade Algebra, where both of them had just aced the first pop quiz of the school year. On the other side of the campus in the upper elementary school building, the fourth, fifth, and sixth graders were exiting their weekly Monday morning assembly. As they filed out, Leah, Maddie, and Rebecca saw each other. As much as they wanted to stop and chat, they knew that talking was not allowed. A wave and a smile would have to do.

Rebecca couldn't wait to get to her first period class—Language Arts. Today was the day she would get to share her paragraph about herself with her class. She also had her *Free to Be Me* Journal, but this was for Mrs. Brown's eyes only. When she had put it in her bookbag that morning, Rebecca wasn't sure how the other kids would react. She thought that they would think her journal was dumb.

Rebecca entered her class and sat down at her desk. As she pulled out her notebook, a pen, and her paragraph, she saw her journal staring back at her. Rebecca sighed and closed her backpack. Mrs. Brown was ready to begin.

"Good morning, students! I'm eager to hear your paragraphs so I can get to know all of you better. Who would like to begin?"

Rebecca did not raise her hand. As much as she loved what she had written, she wasn't ready to share it with the rest of the class. *What if I mess up? I hate dyslexia,* she thought. Rebecca knew she was getting nervous. If she were home, she would look at her happy word painting. That always helped her relax. But she wasn't home. She was in school. *What can I do?* she thought to herself. *I know! Deep breaths…Mom always says take deep breaths.* Rebecca breathed in deeply a couple times and started to feel better. Turning her attention to the front of the room, she began to listen. The second volunteer, Jenny, was reading her paragraph aloud.

Mine is so much better than that! she thought to herself. *I can do this!* Just as Jenny finished reading, Rebecca raised her hand. Mrs. Brown called on her. Standing up, she took one more deep breath and began to read in a loud and confident voice. When she was done, Rebecca realized she had not made even one mistake.

"Excellent, Rebecca!" exclaimed Mrs. Brown. "*Free to be me*…what a wonderful choice of words. What made you think of that?"

Rebecca froze. As much as she wanted to answer Mrs. Brown, she knew she'd have to show everyone her journal.

What if they laugh at me? But she had no choice. Mrs. Brown was waiting.

"My friend, Jordie," said Rebecca.

"Jordie? What do you mean?"

"I'll show you." Rebecca got her journal from her backpack and brought it to Mrs. Brown. "This is my *Free to Be Me* journal. My friend Jordie goes to The Pathways School. Her class has a journal they call *Free to Be Me* because writing their own feelings makes them feel free to be themselves. When she showed it to me, it gave me the idea for my paragraph. I wanted to write about things that make me feel free to be me. When I finished, I decided to make a journal just like Jordie's. My first entry is the paragraph I wrote for you."

Rebecca looked down. She was sure that her classmates were sneering and starting to laugh at her. Just as tears began to well up in her eyes, she heard shouts from all around the room.

"Cool!"

"Can we do that, too?"

"Pass it around, Rebecca!"

Rebecca quickly wiped her tears and looked up. She couldn't believe everyone liked it.

"Settle down, students," said Mrs. Brown. "Let's give everyone a chance to read their paragraphs, and then we can talk about journals. Great idea, Rebecca!"

The rest of the class took their turns reading aloud, but Rebecca did not hear a word. All she could think about were the wonderful things Mrs. Brown and her classmates had said to her. What a way to begin the week.

❦

But Rebecca wasn't the only one having a great day at Royal Palm. In addition to Brayden and Jason, who had gotten 10 out of 10 on their first math quiz of the year, Maddie and Leah felt like they were on top of the world.

In Reading class, Maddie had scored 100% on her first Reading Comprehension test. *Mom was right*, she thought to herself. *Fifth grade reading is gonna be a lot easier this year!*

In fourth grade, Leah's new teacher, Mrs. Chase, had just announced that their class would be doing the Thanksgiving musical presentation for the entire elementary school. It was going to be a show in which the student getting the lead role would need to do gymnastics tricks. Since Leah was the only gymnast in the class, she got the part. *I'm so lucky!* she thought to herself. *Not only do I get to do gymnastics after school, but in school, too!*

The second Monday of the second week of school had turned out to be a really great day.

16
THE TURKEY TUCK

The first three months of the school year passed quickly. When the week of Thanksgiving arrived, no one was more excited than Leah. She had been practicing since the beginning of the school year for her lead role in the Thanksgiving musical called *The Turkey Tuck*. As "Tom Turkey," Leah would be doing all kinds of handsprings, cartwheels, and somersaults to save her turkey friends from becoming Thanksgiving dinner for a very hungry family.

When the last day of school before Thanksgiving break arrived, Leah was ready to go. Dressed in her Tom Turkey costume, she and all her fellow turkey classmates were peeking out from behind the curtain. Leah was so happy. Not only were her parents in the audience, but so were her brother and sister and all the Hoffman kids.

I can't believe Mom and Dad let Jake and Jordie come! she thought. *Everyone's here…Rebecca, Maddie, and even Jason and Brayden.* The Hoffman boys had been given permission to leave Study Hall—their free period to watch her perform. Having her whole family and friends at her show was very important to Leah. Jake and Jordie were always the ones who got all the attention. "It's my turn now," she said aloud, as the curtain began to rise.

For one hour, the fourth-grade performers sang and danced while Leah pranced around the stage doing all kinds of gymnastics to save the turkeys. At the end of the show, the entire audience stood up and could not stop clapping. When Leah stepped forward to take a bow, everyone cheered. She could not believe all this applause was just for her! When the audience settled down and took their seats, Dr. Roberts, Royal Palm's Principal, got up to speak.

"Thank you, fourth grade, for one of the best Thanksgiving shows Royal Palm Academy has even seen. Students and teachers have all done an outstanding job. A special thank you to our Tom Turkey—Leah Green. If this were a gymnastics meet, I'd say you deserved a *Perfect 10!*"

The audience was up on their feet again cheering and applauding. No one was cheering louder than Maddie Hoffman. Dr. Roberts was right. Leah deserved a *Perfect 10*—not only for her gymnastics but also for being the perfect best friend.

When the applause ended, Dr. Roberts continued speaking. "I want to wish all of you a wonderful Thanksgiving. Now, let's all go home and celebrate!"

The students were once again cheering. They couldn't wait to begin their vacation. As the audience began to exit the auditorium, Leah ran off stage, eager to see her family and friends. Mom and Dad got to her first and could not stop hugging her.

"We're so proud of you!" they exclaimed.

"High Fives!' shouted Jordie, Rebecca, Jake, Brayden, and Jason.

"*Perfect 10!*" declared Maddie.

"*Perfect* beginning for a Thanksgiving feast," said Mr. Green.

"No Tom Turkey for me!" Leah exclaimed. "I'll stick to sweet potatoes, veggies, and apple pie!"

"Gobble! Gobble! Gobble!" squawked Jason, while flapping his arms like the wings of a turkey.

"Gobble! Gobble! Gobble!" echoed Jake.

As everyone broke out into laughter, Leah looked on with a big smile. Today she had taken a big leap and *vaulted* to success. Today was *HER* day to shine!

17

BRAG ALERT

Five days later, Thanksgiving break was coming to an end. Although this meant that vacation was over, the Hoffman and Green kids really didn't mind. They had spent so many hours together playing all their favorite indoor and outdoor games and had eaten enough turkey, stuffing, sweet potatoes, veggies, and pie to last a whole year long. Besides, winter break was just around the corner. In three weeks, they would be on vacation again, and this time for fourteen days! But before that would happen, there was a lot to do! They all had to get ready for *The Olympiad*.

Every December, many schools in the community participated in a mega-Olympics, which not only included all kinds of sports but also had competitions in Math, Science, Spelling, Geography, Art, Music, and Drama. Some of the events were open for all students to compete. All you had to do was sign up. Other competitions required students to try out and be selected by a panel of judges who were sent to each participating school. In any case, students were allowed to enter two events, for which there was an entry fee. Parents and students didn't mind because all the money always went to charities for underprivileged children.

The Olympiad was held at a different location each year. This time, Pathways and the nearby community center volunteered to host the competitions. To get things started, each school had scheduled an Olympiad Kickoff Assembly for the very first day after Thanksgiving break. The Hoffman and Green kids couldn't wait!

The Greens were especially excited. This was going to be their first Olympiad. When Jake and Jordie returned to school on Monday morning, there was a lot of buzz in their classroom while everyone waited for the bell to ring.

"We're doing basketball!" Aaron and Noah declared.

"Me, too!" said Jake, running over to join the boys. "21! 21!"

"Not 21," Aaron snapped. "It's Basketball Knockout. Do you even know what that is?"

Jake pulled back. He was an ace at 21 but had never played Knockout. Seeing Jake's discomfort and Aaron's building anger, Miss D stepped in.

"Basketball Knockout!" she exclaimed. "What a fun game! Since you are one of our experts, Aaron, why don't you explain the rules to Jake."

Expert! Aaron thought to himself. His frown turned to a smile. "Okay, Miss D." Aaron turned towards Jake. "It's a foul shot game. Everyone gets a turn to make a shot. If you get the ball in, you stay in line for your next turn. If you miss, you get one more chance. If you miss again, you're out. The player who doesn't miss at all wins. I didn't miss last year, and I won," Aaron said. "And I'm gonna beat everyone again because I'm the best!"

"BRAG ALERT!" Emily said, laughing.

"What's that?" asked Jordie.

"I heard you, Emily," said Aaron. "No BRAG ALERT. Everyone knows I'm the best!"

"Not!" shouted Noah.

"Freeze!" Miss D commanded.

Everyone stopped in their tracks.

"Now all of you take your seats, and do not make a sound; not one sound!"

"But the bell is a sound," said Aaron. "It's gonna ring."

And just then, the 8:20 AM bell sounded.

"I told you," Aaron said, sneering.

Miss D gave Aaron one of her warning looks—the kind of look that meant you'd better stop. But Aaron didn't seem to care. He didn't answer back but continued to sneer at everyone and folded his arms across his chest. Miss D turned towards the rest of the class.

"Last year we spent a lot of time talking about when it's okay to brag and when it's not. Who can remind us of the difference? Emily?"

"If you're proud of something you've done, it's okay to brag about yourself, but just to yourself. You gotta keep it inside your head. If you brag to other kids, it makes you seem better than them."

"That's right, Emily. Jordie, you're next."

"Like what Emily said. In ballet, my teacher tells us to brag to ourselves so we can feel good about what we're doing. That makes us do better. She calls it *self-talk*. But we can never say what we're thinking to other kids. That would be bragging and can hurt them.

"Excellent, Jordie."

"Your turn, Noah."

"Can I say something to Aaron?"

"Yes, Noah, but remember that mean words can hurt, so choose your words carefully."

Noah nodded and turned to Aaron. "You're my best friend, but what you said made me angry. I know you're good at basketball, but you made me feel like I was bad."

Aaron did not respond. Even though he didn't say anything, everyone could tell that Noah's words had gotten to him. His eyes welled up with tears.

"Thank you, Noah," said Miss D. "I know that was hard for you to say. You and Aaron are the best of friends. I'm sure the two of you will work this out like good friends always do. Does anyone else have something to share?"

Emily raised her hand again.

"Can I say something to Aaron, too?"

Miss D. nodded.

"I'm sorry I said BRAG ALERT and laughed. I know that wasn't nice. I won't do that again, Aaron. I made a mistake."

Aaron couldn't believe Emily had apologized. *I was the one who bragged, not her,* he thought. Aaron wiped away his tears, took a deep breath, and raised his hand.

"Yes, Aaron," said Miss D.

Aaron turned towards Noah. "I'm sorry I bragged. I made a mistake, too."

"Well done, Emily and Aaron!" exclaimed Miss D. "I'm so proud of the way you both were able to admit you made mistakes and then apologized. Good job! Now let's move on. It's time for math."

"Wait, Miss D," Ruthie said, while raising her hand.

"Yes, Ruthie?"

"Remember the beginning of school when I said I hated making writing mistakes and then you said mistakes don't have to be a bad thing?"

"Yes...."

"I think I get it now. Aaron and Emily made mistakes. But it's okay they made mistakes cuz we all learned something good from it. Right?"

"Very right, Ruthie!" replied Miss D. "Mistakes are our best teachers. When you realize you've made a mistake, your mistake teaches you a new and different way to act. It takes you on a new path that's better."

"You take us on paths, too, Miss D, cuz we're at Pathways!" joked Aaron.

"Yes, Aaron," Miss D said, chuckling. "And now it's time to explore different paths to make math easier to understand. Please take out your math workbooks and turn to Page 35."

While Miss D got her math lesson started, Jake left the classroom with Miss Ross. Since he excelled in math, Jake was in a different group. Walking to class, he counted his steps and bragged to himself so no one else would hear. *Math Whiz Jake! Math Whiz Jake!* he repeated over and over again. *Self-talk* felt so good just like Jordie said it would.

18

TRYOUTS

On Monday afternoon, the Olympiad officially began. As students left their kickoff assemblies, the only things on their minds were the competitions they wanted to enter. At every school, kids rushed to get in line to make sure they got a space in events that were open to everyone. For competitions that required tryouts, students waited their turns all week long to perform before judges who were sent to each participating school. By the end of the week, the results were in.

Running to the carpool line, Maddie saw Leah. She couldn't wait to tell her.

"I made it!" she shouted. "The judges picked me for gymnastics."

"Me, too!" exclaimed Leah. "I can't believe it!"

"What can't you believe?" asked Rebecca, as she joined the girls.

"We got picked for gymnastics," replied Maddie. "What about you?"

"I made the art contest," said Rebecca. "I have to make a painting about the Olympiad. The best one will go on the cover of the Olympiad magazine."

"Wow!" said Leah. "What kind of stuff goes in that magazine?"

"All the events, the names of everyone who competes, and the winners. I hope that's me!" exclaimed Rebecca.

"Hope so," said Maddie. "And maybe me and Leah will win, too!"

"Win?" asked Brayden.

"Who's winning what?" said Jason.

The boys dumped their backpacks on the pavement and joined the carpool line.

"We all made it!" Rebecca declared. "I'm doing art and Leah and Maddie are doing gymnastics. What about you guys?"

"Just basketball for me," said Jason. "That's all I signed up for. Gotta focus on my foul shots cuz I'm *on the ball,* just like my happy word. When am I getting that?"

"Just as soon as I can," Rebecca replied.

"Guess what I'm doing?" said Brayden.

"Basketball!" the three girls yelled.

"Nope!"

"What do you mean…no?" said Maddie.

A big smile came across Brayden's face. "I got picked for the Spelling Bee again, but this year I want first place. No time for basketball. I gotta practice a lot!"

"Me, too, bro," Jason said. "I guess it'll be up to me to show how we Hoffmans sink those foul shots!"

"What about Jake?" said Leah. "He signed up for basketball, too."

"Jake's the best," replied Jason. "I hope he wins the fifth-grade competition and me, the seventh. Let's call him and Jordie when we get in the car."

Just then, Mrs. Hoffman drove up.

Opening the front door of the minivan, Jason reached in to grab Mom's cell phone. "We gotta call Jake and Jordie and find out what they're doing in the Olympiad."

"Hold on, Jason," Mom said, pulling back her phone. "No need to call them. I just spoke to Mrs. Green. Jake's doing basketball and made it to the math competition. Jordie was picked for ballet."

"Go, Jake!" cheered Jason and Brayden.

"Go, Jordie!" the three girls shouted louder.

"Settle down, kids. You haven't told me what you'll be doing in the Olympiad."

"Okay," replied Jason. "I'm going first."

"I'm next," shouted Brayden.

By the time the last of the kids had finished, Mrs. Hoffman pulled in the driveway.

"I'm so proud of all of you!" Mrs. Hoffman exclaimed.

"Thanks, Mom," said Maddie. "But hold off on the applause. We all have a lot of work to do!"

19

OLYMPIAD PREP

"Knockout Time! Knockout Time," shouted Jake. While waiting for Jason to finish his Sunday morning homework, Jake was practicing his foul shouts in the Hoffman's driveway. Since there were only two weeks until the Olympiad, everyone was in pre-competition training mode.

Jason slammed the front door and ran to the basketball court. "I'm ready, Jake! Let's play ball."

"Knockout Time! Knockout Time!" Jake repeated, as he sunk one foul shot after another.

"Nice, going, Jake! My turn, now."

Jake smiled and threw Jason the ball.

Upstairs in the Hoffman house, Brayden was watching Jake and Jason from his bedroom window. Although he wished he could be outside playing ball, he knew he still had a lot of work to do. Brayden had made a daily practice checklist. On weekdays and Sundays, homework had to be first. So, he allotted one hour to that. Then, he scheduled one more hour for reviewing lists and lists of spelling words.

Although his daily schedule meant there was very little time for playing ball, TV, or video games, Brayden didn't mind and went back to work. He really liked learning how to spell hard words. What really amazed him was how focused he was. For the first time, his mind wasn't wandering at all. When he finished all his work, he put his final mark on his checklist.

Activity	Time	✓
Homework	1 hour	✓
Spelling Bee	1 hour	✓

I can't believe I got everything done! he thought to himself. *Is it possible I could win the Spelling Bee?* Brayden had a big smile on his face but knew that it wasn't a good idea to get his hopes up. He put away his study materials, turned off his computer, and went outside to join Jake and Jason in Basketball Knockout. Just as Brayden got to the court, Jake was leaving with his basketball in hand.

"Hey, Jake. Where are you going?"

"He's got Math Olympiad stuff to do," replied Jason.

"Forty-five minutes basketball…one hour math. Gotta go," said Jake.

When Jake left, Jason continued to shoot foul shots. "Watch me, bro," he said. "I'm on a streak. Twenty-five in a row! Do you think it's possible I could win?"

"Maybe," replied Brayden.

"Twenty-six…twenty-seven…twenty-eight in a row!" Jason shouted. "More than maybe, Brayden. Just watch. I'm gonna do it!"

❧

Watching is just what Rebecca was doing from her open bedroom window. *Jason's really good*, she thought to herself. *Maybe he'll win. Anything's possible. Maybe I'll win!* Rebecca returned to her easel to finish her painting for the Olympiad magazine. Just as she was about to pick up her brush, she closed her eyes. A vision of sleepaway camp flashed before her. Rebecca was back in her bunk getting ready for a big color war game. Her favorite counselor, Stacy, was giving her and her bunkmates a pep talk.

"It's not about winning," Stacy said. "It's about doing your best, being a good sport, and loving every moment from start to finish."

Rebecca's eyes popped wide open. "Stacy's right!" she exclaimed. "I do love every moment!"

Rebecca picked up her brush and began to paint. Time flew by. When she put her final brushstroke on her canvas, she looked at her finished work. "Whether you win or lose," she said aloud, "you should always dream big!" Rebecca smiled. She was proud of herself. Just like Stacy said, she had done her best. You couldn't do better than that.

When Rebecca finished cleaning her brushes and putting away her supplies, she went downstairs. Maddie, Leah, and Jordie had just come back from gymnastics and ballet practice at the community center gym.

"You should've seen me, Rebecca," said Jordie. "The ballet teacher, Miss Nancy, really liked my ballet routine."

"And Coach Jeff said Leah's vault and my floor routine were Perfect 10's!" Maddie exclaimed.

"Do you think we'll all win?" asked Jordie.

"Maybe," Rebecca replied. "Anything is possible."

20

OFF TO THE OLYMPIAD

The two-week pre-competition training period passed quickly. It was now Sunday, and the Olympiad—a three-day event—was about to begin. On Sunday and Monday, all the competitions would take place. On Tuesday, each participating school scheduled assemblies to give out awards.

Students couldn't wait for the Olympiad to start, but they were just as excited for Tuesday to come. Not only was it the awards assembly but it was also a half-day of school followed by winter break. What a way to start vacation!

The Hoffman and Green families were up early. Since there were so many events, the Olympiad was scheduled to start by eight o'clock. When the doorbell rang at 7:15 AM, Jason was already in the front hallway pacing back and forth. Brayden was there, too, practicing spelling words. Opening the door to Jordie, Jake, and Leah, Jason shouted to his mother.

"Let's go, Mom! We can't be late!" The Hoffmans were taking the boys to the Olympiad while the girls carpooled with the Greens.

"Olympiad! 8:00 AM!" Jake shouted. "Can't be late!"

Rebecca came running into the front hallway with two wrapped packages, each tied with a ribbon. "Wait, boys," she yelled. "I have something for you. Maybe it will bring you good luck."

"Good luck?" said Jason. "We could use that."

"Show us what you got, Rebecca," ordered Brayden. "But make it fast."

The boys grabbed the packages and quickly pulled off the ribbons and wrapping paper.

"*Ketchup King!*" exclaimed Brayden, holding up his happy word painting. "My mouth is watering just thinking about the burgers Mom said I could have for dinner tonight. Thanks, Rebecca."

"And I've got *On the Ball*," said Jason. "This is perfect! Just what I needed to get me ready for Knockout!"

On the Ball!

Jason and Brayden placed their happy word paintings on the hall table and walked towards the front door with Jake.

"Let's go, Mom," Jason said again. "Time to show everyone what the Hoffman and Green boys can do!"

"No!" shouted Maddie, as she raced to get to the front door before the boys. "It's time to show what the Hoffman and Green girls can do!"

The four girls laughed and ran out the door behind Maddie. Mr. and Mrs. Green were waiting for them across the street. Meanwhile, Jason, Brayden, and Jake piled into the Hoffman's car.

"Go Hoffmans! Go Greens!" Jake shouted.

"Go Hoffmans! Go Greens!" said Jason and Brayden.

"Go Hoffmans! Go Greens!" echoed Leah, Jordie, Maddie, and Rebecca.

The car doors slammed shut. The Hoffman and Green families were off. The Olympiad was about to begin.

21

THE OLYMPIAD–DAY 1
THE FIRST MORNING

Arriving at Pathways, the Green and Hoffman kids were out of their cars in a flash. Since Basketball Knockout was the first event of the day, Jason and Jake were eager to get to the courts. Grades 4 and 5 were competing at Pathways, and Grades 6–8 at the community center on the same campus.

"Bye, Jake," Jason shouted. "Good luck, buddy!"

Brayden, Rebecca, and Maddie high-fived Jake and ran off with their parents to cheer for Jason at his knockout competition.

"Let's go!" insisted Jake, pulling on both his mom and dad. "Basketball Knockout! 8:00 AM."

Just then, Miss D walked towards the Greens.

"Good morning!" she said.

"Good morning, Miss D."

"Basketball Knockout!" repeated Jake.

"Yes, Jake," said Miss D. "Knockout will be starting in fifteen minutes, but first, it's time for a Coach D pep talk."

"Who's Coach D?" asked Jordie.

"That's me!" Miss D said, winking. "Today and tomorrow, I'm the fifth-grade coach. Follow me!"

Coach D escorted the Green family to the basketball court where all of Jake and Jordie's classmates were waiting on the sidelines.

"Gather around, kids…and parents, too! Today begins the Olympiad. Before you all go off to compete, let's remember why we're here today."

"To win!" yelled Aaron.

"Yes, Aaron," said Coach D. "I'm sure everyone is hoping to win. But what else is important, fifth grade?"

"Sportsmanship!"

"Doing the best you can!"

"Having lots of fun!"

"And helping all the needy children!"

"Excellent," praised Coach D. "All those things are important. But let's go back to what Aaron said first about winning. What if I told you that I think you've already won?"

"How, Coach D?" asked Emily. "The Olympiad hasn't started yet."

"You're right, Emily. It hasn't. But winning isn't always about who has the highest score or who makes the most foul shots. You don't have to beat someone to be a winner. A true winner is someone who does better than he or she did the day before. Think about the last three weeks. What have all of you been doing?"

"Pre-competition training," Jake replied.

"And how has that helped?" asked Coach D.

"We got better," said Emily.

126

"So, if you're better than you were before, what does that mean?"

"We're winners!" they all shouted.

"Exactly! You're already winners. Now I want you to go out there, be good sports, try your best, and have lots of fun. But remember, whether you win or lose, you're already a winner, and that's what really matters!"

The bell rang. It was 8:00 AM. Four judges appeared on the court—two at each basketball hoop. Fourth grade competitors lined up by one hoop and fifth graders at the other.

"Let's play ball," the judges shouted.

Jake was first in line. *Winner Jake*, he thought to himself. *Win or lose, I'm winner Jake!*

✍

The morning passed quickly. By noon, Basketball Knockout, the quarter-mile running dash, the front crawl 25-meter swimming race, and the singles ping pong and tennis tournaments had taken place. As all the competitors and their families sat down at wooden picnic tables to eat lunch, the fields were abuzz with conversation about the outcome of each event.

Some of the kids from Miss D's fifth-grade Pathways class were sitting together. They couldn't believe that three of their classmates had already won awards. Emily, with her very long legs, placed second in the quarter mile dash, and Ruthie won the front crawl 25-meter swimming race. Jake, who was playing Basketball Knockout for the very first time, came in third. Although Noah did not win in basketball, he felt happy for his new friend Jake. Aaron, however, was very angry. Sitting on the edge of the bench facing away from the table, he put his head down and covered his face with his hands.

"I should have won," he muttered. "It's not fair."

Coach D knew that losing at basketball was very difficult for Aaron to handle. Thinking he might need another pep talk, she walked over to the fifth grade table. But Coach D didn't get a chance. Noah, Aaron's best friend, was already there.

"It's okay, Aaron," Noah said gently. "We all know you're the best at Knockout. You taught me to play and even helped Jake. You're like a coach! And just like Coach D said, if we do our best, we're already winners!"

Aaron looked up at Noah and smiled. *Me, a coach?* he thought to himself. *How cool is that!*

"Coach Aaron!" shouted Jake.

"Go, Coach Aaron!" echoed his classmates.

Jake ran off to join his family and all the Hoffman kids. When he got to the table, Jason stood up and gave him a high five.

"Nice going, Jake!" he said. "Brayden and I are proud of you!"

"Winner Jake!" Jake replied.

"What about you, Jason?" Jordie asked. "Did you win Knockout?"

Jason did not respond. He hadn't won and was having a hard time admitting it. Dr. Hoffman came over to him and put his arm around his son's shoulders. With his dad by his side, he answered Jake. "I lost, Jake. But that's okay cuz I tried my best and had a really good time."

Jake closed his eyes and thought about Jason losing and Coach D's morning pep talk. Opening his eyes, he turned to Jason. "Win or lose, you're a winner," he declared. "High fives for Jason!"

22

The Olympiad–Day 1
The First Afternoon

After lunch, it was time for the gymnastics competition. The Green and Hoffman families were sitting on benches in the stands waiting to cheer on Leah and Maddie. When the fourth-grade vault competition was announced, Leah gave her parents a hug and walked to the vault area. While she waited her turn, she dipped her hands in powdered chalk and wiped it on her feet so she wouldn't slip. Leah then closed her eyes and took deep breaths. Visions of her *vault* happy word painting danced in front of her eyes. Win or lose, she knew that if she wanted to succeed, she always had to be willing to *vault*—to take a big leap. Just then, Judge Jenny announced her name.

"Next up is Leah Green from Royal Palm Academy."

Leah's eyes popped open. Moving to the runway, Leah raised one arm above her head to signal she was ready. Then she was off. Leah began to run faster and faster down the runway. She knew she needed speed to give her enough power for her handspring. When she reached the springboard, Leah took a big jump. She put her hands down on the vault and pushed off into her handspring. *Perfect!* she thought to herself, as she flew through the air. All she had to do now was ace her landing.

"THUMP!" Leah fell to the floor. Clutching her ankle, tears came to her eyes. It really hurt. Within seconds, her parents, Judge Jenny, and a doctor were by her side.

"My ankle!" she cried. "I twisted it."

While Mr. and Mrs. Green sat with Leah, the doctor examined her ankle.

"Looks like a sprain," he said. "Nothing that ice, Tylenol, and rest won't fix. But get an x-ray tomorrow to be sure."

"You're going to be fine, Leah," Mom said, soothingly. "I'll take you home so you can rest."

"No!" she cried. "I gotta be here for Maddie and Jordie. Please, Mom!"

Mr. and Mrs. Green looked at each other and at Judge Jenny. Although they all thought it would be better for Leah to go home, they decided to let her stay. Judge Jenny sat down on the floor by Leah and put her arm around her shoulders.

"You should be very proud of yourself," she said. "Even though you fell, I can see that you're an outstanding gymnast with Perfect 10's in your future. But more important than that is how you acted after your injury. You didn't think about yourself. The only thing you wanted to do was be there for other competitors. That's true sportsmanship! How about you sit with me and the other judges for the rest of the afternoon? It would be an honor to have you with us!"

Leah was speechless. All she could do was nod her head. She couldn't believe she was going to get a chance to sit with all the judges and watch Maddie and Jordie perform. Within seconds, Leah was lifted from the floor and carried to the judges' booth, where two chairs had been put together so she could stretch her legs. Everyone cheered for her.

For the rest of the afternoon, Leah iced her ankle while watching all the gymnastic and ballet events. When the first full day of competition ended, the results were in. Maddie came in third in gymnastics, and Jordie got second place in ballet. They were so, so happy. Thinking back to Coach D's early morning pep talk, Leah realized that Coach D was right. *You don't have to beat someone to be a winner.* Even though she didn't get a medal, she felt like she had won. Now she couldn't wait for Monday—the second day of the Olympiad. That's when Brayden would compete in the Spelling Bee and Jake would compete in the Math Whiz contest. Whether they won or lost, the Hoffmans and Greens would be there to cheer them on.

23

THE OLYMPIAD–DAY 2 THE SPELLING BEE

Monday morning arrived. Once again, the Hoffmans and Greens carpooled together for the second day of the Olympiad. Arriving at Pathways, Brayden was out of the car first, as the seventh grade Spelling Bee was scheduled for 9:00 AM.

Brayden ran to the community center auditorium and went up on stage. Four other seventh-grade competitors were there with cards hanging around their necks. Brayden looked at his number five and smiled to himself. *I can do this!* Brayden was confident. He had practiced lists and lists of spelling words over and over again. All he had to do was spell the most words correctly within 45 minutes, and he would be declared the winner.

The seats in the auditorium filled up. From the stage, Brayden saw the Greens as well as his entire family waving at him. The lights dimmed in the auditorium. The judge spoke to the contestants.

"Welcome, students. When I call your number, I will give you a word and use it in a sentence. You will need to repeat the word, spell it correctly, and then repeat the word again. Good luck to all of you."

The clock was started, and Round 1 of the Spelling Bee began. All five students spelled their first words correctly. Next was Round 2, then Rounds 3, 4, and 5. No one was making a mistake. The score was tied. *These kids are good*, Brayden thought. But…by the time Round 10 was over, there were only two students left—Contestant Number 1, a girl named Jessica, and Brayden.

"Round 11!" the judge announced. "This may be our last round, as time is running out. Time to move onto our challenge words!"

Brayden knew the words were going to get much harder. Jessica stepped up and looked really scared.

"The word is *pediatrician*. Mom took her sick little boy to the *pediatrician*."

"Pediatrician," said Jessica. "P-E-D-I-A-T-R-I-C-A-N. Pediatrician."

"I'm sorry," said the judge. "That is incorrect." The correct spelling is *P-E-D-I-A-T-R-I-C-I-A-N*. Good try!"

Jessica was escorted off the stage. Brayden was the only one left, and time was running out. He had to get his word right. If not, the Spelling Bee would be a tie! Brayden stepped forward.

"The word is *ophthalmologist*. The *ophthalmologist* examined my eyes."

Brayden pulled on his glasses and smiled. He knew this word so well. Since the time he was three months old, he had been going to Dr. Pratt, his favorite ophthalmologist.

"Ophthalmologist," said Brayden. "O-P-H-T-H-A-L-M-O-L-O-G-I-S-T. Ophthalmologist."

"Correct! The winner is Contestant Number 5—Brayden Hoffman!"

The audience was up on their feet clapping and cheering, with the Hoffmans and Greens the loudest of them all. Brayden was beaming. He couldn't wait to see his family and friends. But first, he had to congratulate the other contestants. Sportsmanship always came first. When he was done, everyone was waiting for him.

"I did it!" he exclaimed.

"You certainly did," said Dr. Hoffman.

"Winner Brayden," Jake shouted.

"Thanks, Jake," replied Brayden. "But all the spellers were just as good as me. I got lucky with the word *ophthalmologist*. That's an easy one for me. Right, Mom?"

Yes, Brayden," said Mom. "But you're still the winner. Not only because you won the Spelling Bee but because of your hard work and good sportsmanship. Dad and I are very proud of you!"

"Thanks, Mom."

"Math Time!" shouted Jake. "Gotta go!"

"Good luck, Jake!" Jason yelled.

Math Whiz Jake was on the move.

24

The Olympiad–Day 2
The Math Competition

Jake arrived at the Pathways Computer lab where twenty-four other fifth grade students from many different schools were getting settled at their seats. Part 1 of the math competition was about to begin. Each of them would have to take a thirty-minute online math test with 30 multiple choice questions. The five students who got the highest scores on this test would move on to the Lightning Round.

Jake sat down at a computer and watched the clock. *9:57 AM*, he thought. *Three more minutes.* When the buzzer went off, the computer lab became silent except for the clicking sounds on the contestants' keyboards. Time passed quickly. When the buzzer sounded to end the test, the students were surprised. Thirty minutes seemed like thirty seconds.

"Time's up!" the judge called. "All hands down!"

While the judge tallied the results at his computer, students whispered at their seats—but not Jake. He was frozen. Knowing he had to be quiet while waiting for the results, he talked to himself. Self-talk really helped him to keep calm. *Win or lose, I'm winner Jake!* he repeated over and over again. But Jake did not have to wait long.

"I have the results," the judge announced. "The five students who will be going to the Lightning Round are...."

As the judge called out the names of other student winners, Jake put his hands over his ears. The only name he wanted to hear was his own.

"And the final contestant will be... Jake Green!"

Jake jumped up and moved quickly to the front of the room where the judge handed him his ticket.

"On to the Lightning Round," the judge shouted.

Jake and his four math competitors ran out of the computer lab. Outside the door, the Hoffmans and the Greens were waiting.

"I got it!" shouted Jake, while waving his ticket for all of them to see.

"Pathways auditorium here we come," said Jason. "Jake's turn to show his stuff!"

Arriving at the auditorium, Jake ran up on stage. He found his seat at the contestants' table where lots of paper and pencils had been placed. He was Contestant Number

Three. Next to the table was a large Smartboard. When the Lightning Round began, each math problem would be projected on the screen for all the contestants and the audience to see.

The auditorium filled up quickly. The judge walked up to the microphone, and everyone got quiet.

"Welcome to our annual fifth grade Math Competition. Today, we have five contestants who have made it to our Lightning Round. This round will last thirty minutes. For each question, the student who gets the correct answer first wins the point. At the end of thirty minutes, the student with the most points will be the winner. Good luck, contestants!"

The judge started the clock, and the competition began. The first question flashed on the screen. He read it aloud.

$$\text{"}(7 \times 2) + 10 \times 0 = ?\text{"}$$

Contestant Number Two buzzed first. "0!"

"That is correct. One point for Contestant Number Two." The judge went to the second question.

"What number of eggs is the average of one dozen plus two dozen?"

"18!" said Contestant Number One.

"Correct! A point for Contestant Number One!"

The judge read three more math questions, but Jake did not get to the buzzer quick enough. In the audience, the Greens and Hoffmans were sitting on the edges of their seats. So were Coach D and Jake's grade five classmates.

"Come on, Jake!" Jordie and Emily whispered.

"Math Whiz Jake!" Noah and Aaron repeated to themselves.

"Question number six," the judge announced.

"What time is 120 minutes before 4 PM?"

Jake's buzzer went off instantly. No one knew time better than Jake.

"2:00 PM!" shouted Jake.

"Exactly," replied the judge. "A point for Contestant Number Three."

Jake was back in the game. By the time the bell sounded to end the competition, thirty questions had been asked. The judge announced the results for the three highest scores.

"In third place, with a score of 6, is Contestant Number Two—Talia Gold! In second place, with seven questions correct, is Contestant Number One—Joe Miller! And in first place, with the highest score of eight questions correct, is Contestant Number Three—Jake Green!"

Cheers erupted all over the auditorium.

"Go, Jake!" shouted all the Greens and Hoffmans.

"Go, Jake!" echoed his classmates. Jake was their hero. No student from the Pathways Learning Center had ever won the Math Competition.

When the cheering died down, Jake started to walk off stage but then stopped in his tracks. He remembered what Brayden had done when he won the Spelling Bee. Jake walked back on stage towards the four other contestants. "Good job!" he repeated, as he shook each of their hands.

Coach D and his classmates were all waiting for him when he came off stage.

"We're all so proud of you," Coach D. exclaimed. "Tell him why, fifth grade!"

"Good sportsmanship!" yelled Aaron and Noah.

"Had lots of fun!" exclaimed Emily.

"Tried his best!" said Ruthie.

"Did his best!" Jordie declared.

"Math Whiz Jake!" they all shouted.

"Math Whiz, indeed," exclaimed Coach D. "But Jake's not the only one who's a whiz. I'm proud of all of you! Whether you came in first, second, third, or not all, you're all…"

"WINNERS!" they shouted. "And that's what really matters!"

25

THE AWARDS ASSEMBLY

The Olympiad was just about over. For the rest of the day, the Hoffman and Green kids cheered on their friends and classmates in the remaining events. Since their competitions were over, they felt relieved—everyone except Rebecca. Even though she was very happy that Maddie, Jordie, Jake, and Brayden had won, she still didn't know whether she had won a medal, too. It was the last day of the Olympiad, and the results of the art contest had not been announced. Whose painting would be on the cover of the Olympiad magazine? That was a question that would not be answered until the Olympiad Awards Assembly the very next day. Tuesday morning could not come soon enough!

❧

When her cell phone alarm went off on Tuesday morning, Rebecca was already dressed. She couldn't wait to get to school.

"Jason, Brayden, Maddie," she shouted. "You gotta get up!" Running to each of their rooms, she was surprised to find that there were all up and dressed, too.

"Chill, Rebecca," said Brayden. "Of course we're up. Do you think we're gonna be late for the awards assembly?"

"No way!" replied Maddie. "Can't wait to get my medal!"

Maddie ran to the stairway. Passing by Rebecca, she stopped suddenly when she noticed tears in her sister's eyes. "Don't worry, Rebecca," she said. "Nobody paints like you. You have to win the art contest!"

Just then, Jason came out of his room with his arms behind his back.

"What's in your hands, bro?" asked Brayden.

"A gold medal for Rebecca!" he exclaimed, as he handed her one of the gold ribbons he had won at camp. "Win or lose, you deserve first prize for the best happy word paintings ever!"

"Thanks, Jason," she said. Wiping her tears, Rebecca suddenly began to laugh. Jason always knew how to make her feel better.

"Let's go, kids!" Mrs. Hoffman shouted. "Breakfast time. We don't want to be late for the last day of school before winter vacation."

The Olympiad Awards Assemblies began at participating schools all over the community. At 9:00 AM, Jake, Jordie, and their fifth-grade classmates received their medals at Pathways while Mr. and Mrs. Green stood by and watched proudly. Younger sister Leah watched, too, although she had crutches to keep weight off her sprained ankle.

At 11:00 AM, grades 4–8 students at Royal Palm Academy were all assembled in their auditorium. When Maddie and Brayden were given their gold medals for gymnastics and spelling, Jason, Rebecca, and their parents cheered loudly. As the assembly drew to its conclusion, Dr. Roberts, Royal Palm's Principal, rolled out a covered painting on an easel.

"It's now time to reveal the name of the student whose painting will be placed on the front of our Olympiad magazine. On this easel is a copy of the painting that has been selected. I am proud to say that for the very first time, the winner is one of our school's students. Will Grade 6 student Rebecca Hoffman come forward to reveal this year's magazine cover?"

Rebecca was shocked. She couldn't believe this was really happening. Students from so many schools had submitted paintings, but hers was the one that had been chosen. As she walked on the stage, everyone was applauding.

"Okay, Rebecca," said Dr. Roberts. "Time for the big reveal!"

Rebecca took off the cover. Gasps could be heard throughout the room. Her artwork was amazing. Everyone stood up and began to cheer and stomp their feet.

Dream Big!

As the school photographer took her picture with her painting, her parents, along with Jason, Brayden, and Maddie, were escorted to the stage. A special award like this deserved a family picture, too.

After posing for the photo, Rebecca looked out into the audience. There she saw Jordie and her whole family cheering and waving their hands. *I can't believe they're here!* she thought to herself.

The Awards Assembly ended, and the Hoffmans descended from the stage. Waiting for them were the Greens. Rebecca and Maddie ran over to hug Jordie and Leah.

"How come you're here?" asked Rebecca.

"Surprise!" shouted Jordie.

"What about your Awards Assembly?" said Maddie.

"It was over by ten," Jordie replied. "So, Mom and Dad said we could come watch yours."

"We're so happy your painting got picked," said Leah. "You really are the best!"

148

"And all of you are the best, too," exclaimed Rebecca. "The Greens and the Hoffmans—BFF's! Best friends forever!

"BFF's," shouted Jake!

"BFF's," echoed Brayden, Jason, Maddie, Jordie, and Leah.

The Hoffman and Green kids had all dreamed big, and so many of their dreams had come true. As Rebecca got into bed on the first night of winter break, she put her head down on her pillow and took one last look at her *different* happy word painting shining in the moonlight peeking through her window. Closing her eyes, she yawned and whispered, "Anything is possible!"

THANK YOU NOTES

ॐ First, I want to thank my four children—Benjamin Wander, Robin Sherman, Joshua Wander, and Mollie Wander. The four books of my *Triple Trouble Plus One* series would never have been written if it weren't for them! Although these novels are works of fiction, the personalities of the Hoffman foursome are based on my own triplets plus one more when they were children.

ॐ Although *Anything is Possible* is a work of fiction, the story is in large part based on my many experiences as a teacher, principal, and educational consultant in school settings. In addition to my own background knowledge, I am indebted to administrators, teachers, parents, and students of two schools in particular: *Kesher* in North Miami Beach, Florida—a school for students with learning disabilities and developmental delays and *Nativ* at the *Scheck Hillel Community School* in North Miami Beach, Florida—a program for students with dyslexia and related learning disabilities.

- Thank you Dr. Ezra Levy, Kesher Head of School, and Eileen Ginzburg, Kesher Assistant Director and Scheck Hillel Community School Director of Academic Programs. These two amazing educators opened the doors to their schools and allowed me to visit their classrooms, meet with teachers, talk with students, and contact parents. Moreover, they were my first editors. Their keen insights helped me more accurately depict student and teacher inter-actions in these two schools.

- Thank you, Kayla Levy, Kesher Middle School Coordinator, and Melissa Burger, Kesher Lower School Coordinator, for sharing with me the unique academic, social, and emotional journeys of lower and middle school students. I appreciate all the time you spent with me to enhance my understanding of Kesher children.

- Where would any student be without a very dedicated staff of teachers? I was so fortunate to meet with a number of them many times and visit their classrooms.

  - At Nativ, thank you to Grades 3–4 teacher Mazal Oberlender and Grade 5 teacher Ana Yativ.

  - At Hillel, thank you to Grade 4 Science teacher Mrs. Jessica Salzberg for inviting me into her class where Nativ students had been mainstreamed.

  - At Kesher, thank you to Melissa Levy, Kesher Behaviorist, who invited me into her grades 4–5 social skills class, as well as Adriana Lemor, whose middle school social-emotional learning class I also observed. So enlightening!

  - A very special thank you to Grades 4–5 Kesher teacher, Katura Trapp. I can't count the number of times I met with Katura, visited her classroom, and communicated with her by email. Katura was a great resource and also made some wonderful suggestions after reading the first few chapters of my first draft. I am so appreciative of all the time she was always willing to give me no matter how busy her schedule.

- My understanding of the needs of children with learning differences was also enhanced by my interviews with two parents with children in Kesher and Nativ. Thank you, Chana Kagan and Russell Lazega, for taking the time to speak with me. Your important messages that *everyone should appreciate their own unique qualities* and that *different does not mean less* resonate throughout my book.

- The most heartwarming feedback I received came from three Kesher students. When asked what messages they would like my book to impart to other students, here is what they shared.

  - Dov Szniger (Grade 7): *Never give up on what you do. Don't give up your dreams!*
  - Chaya Kagan (Grade 8): *Even though we're behind, it will all even out in the end. If we give our best, we'll be successful.*
  - Aaron Traub (Kesher alumnus—Univ. of Maryland student): *Don't compare yourself to others...don't live in the past...look forward!*

Thank you Dov, Chaya, and Aaron for meeting with me and sharing your very profound thoughts. All your messages were driving forces as I wrote *Anything is Possible*.

❧ Thank you to Ellen Brazer, published author of two novels and one non-fiction book. For each book in the *Triple Trouble Plus One* series, Ellen has been my sounding board. I am so grateful for all the time she spent with me as I read aloud each and every one of my books. Her suggestions greatly enhanced each novel in this series. Thank you, Ellen, for being my writing mentor. More importantly, thank you for always being there for me. Your friendship is truly a blessing!

❧ As many times as an author revises and edits a novel, it is never enough. Professional advice is always needed. I am fortunate that I was able to turn for the fourth time to Integrative Ink Editing and Publishing Services, who added the final touch with their superb editing, book design, and layout of this novel. Thank you to Editor Stephanee Killen for her time, effort, and professional expertise.

❧ Finally, I would like to thank my husband, Stephen. You have always been my greatest supporter, quietly encouraging me from the sidelines. As we reach our milestone 40th wedding anniversary, I want to express my love and infinite gratitude to you for helping me to realize each and every one of my dreams. With you by my side, ***anything is possible***!

ABOUT THE ILLUSTRATOR

Carlos Alvarez Cotera is a Cuban born artist who lives and works in Gastonia, North Carolina. His passion for art began with drawing when he was a very young child. As a professional artist for the past nineteen years, he has experimented with all kinds of materials, including pencil, watercolor, acrylic, oil, clay, glass, tiles, and even jewelry making! Mr. Cotera spends most of his time with painting. According to him, *"Art is what I was born to do."* Not only does he create amazing works of art, but he also loves to teach students. Carlos Alvarez Cortera says, *"It is a privilege to teach others and help them improve their abilities and see what has become second nature to me."*

Mr. Cotera is credited with creating the drawings of Jake, Jordie, and Leah Green—three new characters introduced in this novel as well as the front cover art. His illustration of children reaching to the stars beautifully conveys the message that *anything is possible*!

CPSIA information can be obtained
at www.ICGtesting.com
Printed in the USA
LVHW030850230920
666817LV00001B/115

9 780997 055870